Carissa Ann Lynch is a *USA Today*-bestselling author. She resides in Floyds Knobs, Indiana with her husband, children, and collection of books. She's always loved to read and never considered herself a "writer" until a few years ago when she couldn't find a book to read and decided to try writing her own story. With a background in psychology, she's always been a little obsessed with the darker areas of the mind and social problems.

carissaannlynch.wordpress.com

 facebook.com/CarissaAnnLynchauthor
twitter.com/carissaannlynch

D0170090

WHISPER ISLAND

CARISSA ANN LYNCH

One More Chapter
a division of HarperCollins*Publishers*
1 London Bridge Street
London SE1 9GF

www.harpercollins.co.uk

HarperCollins*Publishers*
1st Floor, Watermarque Building, Ringsend Road
Dublin 4, Ireland

This paperback edition 2021

2

First published in Great Britain in ebook format
by HarperCollins*Publishers* 2021

A catalogue record of this book is available from the British Library

ISBN: 978-0-00-842106-9

Printed and bound in Great Britain by
CPI Group (UK) Ltd, Croydon CR0 4YY

Dedicated to my family

"We are like islands in the sea, separate on the surface but connected in the deep."

— William James

Watch Me

The backbone of every triumph is built on two simple words: *Watch me.*

Like when my parents said I'd never make it to graduation, I whispered those words: *Watch me.*

And from that day forward, I never got in trouble at school. Never made another bad mark in class. Not because I believed them, but because I wanted to prove them wrong.

I'll prove so many people wrong.

Watch me.

When college after college rejected me, and a school counselor suggested that I might consider a different track, I shouted the words "Watch me!" to an empty hall of lockers and doors.

There are many more examples.

But all that matters is NOW.

Six of us are going to the island. Only one of us will make it back.

That one of us will be ME.

From the back of my mind came a familiar, snarky voice: *If you do this, you'll never leave that island. You'll never make it home again.*

But that voice was wrong, and I hadn't had a "home" in years.

As I stared in the mirror, eyes like two gaping holes staring back at me, I didn't say the words this time.

I didn't need to.

They were seared in my brain, writing themselves, like the unseen stylus of an Etch'n'Sketch engraving the words, deep and thick, across my cerebrum.

They rattled like a mantra, growing louder and louder, until they beat like a metal drum.

My lips moved silently in the mirror.

Watch me. Watch me. Watch me.

How It Started

Chapter One

Riley

S ome might say we went too far.

   After all, our plan was born in the span of one drunken weekend. Settled over shots of tequila.

But if you had to credit *one* person—or blame them— then I guess that one person was me. Ultimately, I was the one obsessed with puzzles.

I didn't want to hang out with them in the first place; just the mere junction of words like "group" and "project" gave my introverted ass an ulcer. I avoided people in college, determined to get the work done and get back to my lonely apartment.

But then there was Scarlett. Everything changed after Scarlett.

She was my bridge to the others, extrovert to my

introvert. Follower of all things art and art-drama related, Scarlett had followed the same track as me since freshman year. We shared the same three courses on Tuesdays and an early Foundation studio lesson on Thursdays.

If not for her annoying charm and persistence, our friendship probably never would have gained traction. In fact, I *know* it wouldn't have, because there's no way I would have initiated one in the first place.

I'd always been a loner, having fewer friends than I could count on one hand.

When I went to college, I never expected that I'd make a friend, much less more than one of them. Certainly not friends as glamorous as Scarlett, Sammy, and Mia.

"Riley, right? With an *i* or a *y*?" asked the girl with the bright red hair and million-dollar smile. Her hair was twisted into galactic spirals around her freckled face. She wore fake lashes and blood-red lipstick that was often smudged on her straight white teeth. She had a nice smile; the sort of smile you see in toothpaste commercials.

"Riley with an *i*," I stammered, watching curiously as she plopped down in the seat beside me. Before I could get a word in edgewise, she launched into a noisy monologue about two influencers in the art world who were up in arms on Twitter.

When the girl named Scarlett—of course I knew her name before she told me; it was impossible not to know a person that loud—was done talking, she drew in a deep breath then asked: "So, whose side are you on? 'Cause this shit is important to me when choosing friends." She winked and smiled, something playful but serious behind that cutesy facade. Still, I got the sense that she meant it. I had no clue who these influencers were, and I didn't mess around on Twitter.

Scarlett had a big dimple on her left cheek which reminded me of my first, and only, friend in school. Her name was Sierra—"like the desert, not the singer"—and she'd treated me terribly. Just the thought of that bitch made me clench my jaw.

I cleared my throat, considering the five-minute soap opera Scarlett had dropped on my lap just then. There was obviously a correct answer here, but I wasn't sure what it was.

It was a dispute over plagiarism—one artist claiming another's work too closely resembled their own. *Nothing new in the art world.*

But both artists were clearly respected and well-known, according to Scarlett. I should know about this, but I didn't.

"Truthfully? I'd have to see both pieces to make a fair judgment," I said and shrugged.

When you don't know the answer, just tell the truth. That's an adage I've always lived by, and it usually works out. Not always, but often.

Scarlett's eyes widened. "Excuse me? You haven't actually seen *The Donovans* yet? Where the hell have you been, Rye?"

I wasn't a big fan of nicknames. But I found, coming

from her, "Rye" sounded kind of ... endearing. *Sierra never would have called me "Rye", that's for damn sure.*

"I'm not much on social media," I admitted. Another painful truth-bomb. "I used to have an online journal, but I kept it mostly private..."

Scarlett stared at me, bug-eyed and silent, like she was seeing me for the first time, an exotic animal at the boring old petting zoo.

"Wow. Just ... wow. You don't know what you're missing. The drama on social media alone is worth it, but the connections, Rye ... the connections are everything in this business. It's important to know who's who ... what's trending ... well, don't worry. I'll show you the pics after class so you can see what I'm talking about. I need to know whose side you're on and then I'll know if we can be friends." There it was again: the wink-y smile, making me instantly feel at ease. There was something about her I liked, even though we were nothing alike.

"Okay, sure," I said, laughing awkwardly. I couldn't help feeling embarrassed, always out of the loop and in the dark about all things current on the art scene. It wasn't the first time I'd heard the speech about "connections". Nowadays, my classmates were already building their online presence, some going so far as to sell digital services or be commissioned to do pieces already. But, for me, it was less about connecting and pursuing fame, and more about stroking a compulsion. I'd lived with obsession for decades.

I didn't do art because I wanted to; I did it because I *had* to.

When I tried to imagine my future after college, walking out of those doors with a diploma in Fine Arts, I couldn't see my art displayed on the walls of some fancy exhibition... *Maybe I'll teach.*

But the thought of standing in front of a classroom, even a small one, was terrifying.

No. That's not an option either.

"Hey, I hope I didn't hurt your feelings. I admire it. You're all about the art, glory be damned. Fuck what the powers that be are saying or doing..." Scarlett nudged me.

A flicker of a smile must have shown on my face.

"Yep. I was right about you," Scarlett teased. Before I could ask what she meant by that, she was inviting me to lunch.

Lunch, for me, usually involved grabbing a quick sandwich in the commons, then hiking the mile back to my car, where I would sit in the AC and scarf down my food, hurrying to start the trek back across campus to my last afternoon class. There was a cafeteria in the commons and an outdoor patio, but I never knew where to sit. I preferred eating alone in my car, anyway.

"Okay. I don't think I've ever seen you in the commons before, though," I said, skeptically.

Scarlett released a bellyful of laughter, loud and snort-worthy, catching the attention of classmates nearby. We were all waiting wearily for Mr. McDaniel to show up for class; he was often late, sometimes drunk, and he liked to keep us over while he finished his lesson, as though he had no concept of time.

"Nah, silly. Nobody eats in that shithole! There's this Irish pub downtown, a few blocks from campus, and Tuesdays are dollar beer days."

I thought about my next class, less than forty-five minutes after lunch. *Would I be able to make it back in time?* I hadn't missed a class all semester. But one thing that reassured me: Scarlett was in my next class. If she had to be back on time, then surely, she would make sure we both were.

So that's how it started.

Trailing behind her in the school parking garage, I was happy to climb in the passenger seat of her yellow Mini Cooper, Billie Eilish blaring all the way to the Irish pub, O'Malley's on 11th Street, nestled between a boarded-up bookstore and a hemp shop.

When Scarlett told the hostess that two more were coming, I couldn't hide my surprise and disappointment. As an introvert, it was hard enough connecting with one person, let alone three.

"Don't worry. Sammy and Mia are cool. You're going to love them, I promise," Scarlett said, as though she could sense the bubble of anxiety that lived under my skin. *It's always there, brewing and bubbling, waiting to be squeezed until it explodes from within.*

But in the end, Scarlett was right. Mia and Sammy were cool, and I was excited, in particular, to meet Mia.

After that day, afternoons at O'Malley's became a regular thing, even sometimes on our days off from classes. It was a tiny, claustrophobic space with slabs of wood for tables and the faint smell of beer and piss embedded in the mothball-colored carpet.

But it was less about the atmosphere and more about the company. These three women intrigued the hell out of me.

Mia, with her feathery black hair dipped in blue, her shapeless paint-stained tops, she wore the uniform of "artist" well. She was gorgeous, stunning even, with the type of beauty that seems reckless and easy. The kind that feels unfair.

Sammy was different. Neatly pressed, she often sported button-down shirts and starched khakis, never a hair out of a place in her neat brown bob. She wore thick black glasses. No makeup. Despite her lengthy school hours, she maintained the books for a popular smoke shop in town, and I could often smell the tangy aroma of nicotine on her hands. I still wasn't sure why she chose art instead of accounting. She liked numbers and she was the most organized of the group. Scarlett joked once that Sammy was our "Velma" of the group, which of course made her our "Daphne", seeing as she was the only redhead of the gang.

Mia and I had looked at each other then. "If they're Velma and Daphne, who's that make us?" she'd teased. We were both dark-headed, Mia and I, but unlike her with her natural, fuck-it-why-try beauty and strange blue stripes, I had to work hard just to look presentable with my thinning hair and ruddy complexion. The extra pounds I'd been carrying for months didn't help either. *The freshman fifteen*, they called it. More like the "freshman fifty" for me.

"I guess we're Scooby Doo and Shaggy, unless you want to be Fred?" I had teased, surprising myself when I got a laugh out of her. *Hell, maybe I can do this friend thing after all.* Mia had a great laugh; she would tilt her head back and open her lips as wide as they would go, then laugh from her belly.

Mia had taken an instant liking to me, which pleased me more than I cared to admit.

It was silly, the way the four of us acted. Getting sloshed during the middle of a weekday, cracking jokes about cartoons that showed our age, and listening to Scarlett's latest online gossip as though it were gospel. She liked to joke that Tuesdays were "church": "Come listen to me speak now, children," she often joked, taking the pulpit behind a table in a corner booth, lining up rows of tequila and bottles of beer.

But it was fun. Hell, it was so fun that I didn't mind missing the occasional class or being late anymore. I enjoyed feeling part of the "gang", even if it was only during school hours.

Mia was a painter, and the second she had walked in the pub, on that first day, I recognized her. How could I not have put two and two together? Mia was THE Mia Ludlow. Daughter of Cristal Ludlow, the famous local sculptor and painter whose work was easily recognized all over the country, and even internationally. But it wasn't just her mother's legacy that made me recognize her: no, Mia's work stood for itself. She had been spotlighted many times all over campus, and in some local papers as well. She was already well regarded in the art world because of her mother, but the work itself justified the attention. *Destined to outdo her mother*, one headline had read, featuring a nightmarish portrait of Jesus she had made on lithograph paper.

But according to Scarlett, there was more to Mia than met the eye. More than the talent and the famous name— she had a reputation. Everyone knew that scandal followed the rich girl, but nobody seemed to care.

Sammy and Mia, despite looking and acting like polar opposites, had been friends since grade school, growing up in Cement Ville together and competing against one another in local art contests and fairs. Now, they were no longer rivals, but best friends and roommates, they liked to proclaim.

Sammy liked to keep Mia's humility in check. "Oh, get over yourself, Mia," she often teased, rolling her eyes and smirking as Mia shared photos of her current works in progress, a dilapidated version of Monroe Institute, our school. It resembled the campus, buildings and landmarks easily recognizable, but everything was lopsided and distorted, the upside-down, creepy version of real life. And it was done in dark gray acrylic paint.

Mia had this style beyond compare; she took normal everyday objects and destinations and turned them into hideous versions of themselves. For me, viewing her art was like seeing my own soul on display, although I'd never admit that to her.

When you live with anxiety and depression, it alters the view on everything. Looking at her work made me feel seen; there's no other way to explain it.

All her work was hauntingly beautiful and a little disorganized, like Mia herself.

"Mia's a genius," Scarlett explained that first day (although I already knew that, as I'd been following her work on campus and in the papers for years). "We love her, but she's always in her own head, working through next steps, planning her next project... We like to keep her in the present, and of course keep her humble." Scarlett winked across the table at Sammy. We all knew Mia had gotten into some trouble in her freshman year of college and she'd had to come back and do her freshman hours all over again ... but we never talked about that. I waited for the others to bring it up, but they never did. Her talent and legacy overshadowed any of the hidden parts of herself...

All three were different, yet there was something about each of them... Mia's careless beauty and dark genius. Sammy's snarky jokes and studious, know-it-all attitude. And of course, Scarlett, with her gossip and wink-y smiles.

The girls didn't kiss each other's asses, but I could tell they were close; teasing often, but in a way that you knew meant love.

I couldn't help wanting a small piece of that for myself.

By the time our sandwiches and beers showed up that day, it was half past noon. Still nervous about the time, I drank my beer too quickly, feeling loose in the lips and warm to the touch within minutes of receiving my meal.

"There's no way we'll get back on time," I told Scarlett. *Is that a slight slur in my voice?* I had wondered, cringing.

"No worries, Rye. We'll just have a couple more, then finish our food. We'll be twenty minutes late, tops, I promise. And, hey, what does Grossman care anyway? It's not like he takes roll. Plus, it's college. We pay for these stupid classes. We shouldn't have to go to every single one if we don't want to," Scarlett said.

"Huh. I never thought of it like that," I burped, slugging down another beer. It tasted awful and flat, lukewarm on my tongue, but at that point, I didn't care.

As usual, Scarlett was right. Grossman didn't notice when we snuck in late that day, or any other day after. She flirted with him, batting those hideous, spidery lashes, and he always let us slide. I quickly learned that Scarlett didn't follow rules—as fun as she seemed, she was also impulsive. A few days into our friendship, I found her in the bathroom on campus, crushing up a pill with a razor. She snorted the entire thing in one fell swoop, then offered to chop me a line.

I shook my head and said, "No, thank you."

As the weeks went on, our Tuesday lunches turned into a regular thing. I stopped worrying about being late and started worrying about my friends. It's not that I was lonely or desperate for friends—the opposite, actually. The degree with which these women intrigued me was baffling, even to me.

Mia wasn't the only genius in the group. Over time, I learned more about Sammy and Scarlett's passions as well. Sammy had a knack for computers and graphic design, creating some of the most incredible images; you'd never know they weren't sketched by hand. And Scarlett, for all her talk of gossip and scandal, and her small drug problems, had quite the impressive social media following. I didn't sign up for Instagram, but I googled her. Nearly 50k followers, and she posted day and night. Discussing technique and the latest trends in the art world; she always had something to say that drew people in. Did she create her own art, or spend all her time talking about it? I often wondered if it mattered anymore. She had a way with people—a skill so foreign to me, I'd prefer to recreate the Sistine Chapel than try to imitate Scarlett's presence online.

Weeks became months, and somehow, the friendships continued until the end of the semester, much to my surprise and delight.

I'm not sure how our hangouts evolved from weekly lunch sessions into weekend sleepovers... Well, that's not true. *I do.*

Again, it started with me. My suggestion.

"Tomorrow is Friday, y'all. Got any big plans?" Scarlett had asked one Thursday afternoon. We were piled into our normal booth in the back of the pub. The table was dirty, elbows sticking to the plastic placemats. Sammy, as usual, set to work, using her own pack of disinfectant wipes to clean off her space.

Scarlett nudged me, hard, in the ribs. "What are you doing this weekend, Rye?"

I tried to imagine how Scarlett spent her weekends. Images of that straw in her hand, residue fringing her nostrils, came to mind. I shrugged.

For them, weekends probably meant freedom and fun. For me, they were lonely. I looked forward to weekdays because I got to attend classes and see them, although admitting that seemed rather loser-ish now.

"Probably going to finish my puzzle," I said, finally. Normally, I wouldn't have brought up my puzzle craze, but I was tired, and too depressed about the impending weekend to care.

I expected them to laugh at me. After all, who spends their time doing puzzles? *Little old ladies, that's who*, I could imagine my old friend Sierra saying.

"Oh, damn. I love puzzles. I haven't done one in, like, I don't know … a decade," Mia exclaimed.

"Me neither," Sammy chimed in as she smudged the disinfectant wipe in a slow, methodical circle. "I like doing them online sometimes. Have you guys tried that puzzle photo app? You can take any of your photos and turn them into puzzles, then work them online…"

"Nah. I'd rather do a real puzzle. And a hard one too, like ten thousand pieces," Scarlett said, signaling for our waiter to bring another round of shots.

"You all should come over to my place. We could do a puzzle together," I said, an edge of hopefulness in my tone. It was like someone else talking, the words not my own. *Did I really just invite these girls over to my place—my tiny apartment with no working windows and few personal effects—to do puzzles together?*

I'd imagined inviting Mia over a thousand times, and the others too, but never this soon. And not like this.

"Hell yeah. I'm down. How about tomorrow?" Scarlett suggested.

Chapter Two

Mia

When the girl said she liked doing puzzles, that was a serious understatement.

Riley's apartment was a little weird, I must admit, small and cavernous—she had explained the windows were incredibly old, the kind you have to twist a crank to get open. Unfortunately, none of the cranks were working and she said they were too expensive to fix. Plus, it was hot, with very little air coming in or out.

I couldn't imagine living in that tomb, honestly.

No natural sunlight or fresh air. Yikes.

How does she ever get any sun? I couldn't help wondering.

Despite the lack of space, the apartment was neat and orderly, only a few personal touches on the walls. But I had to say, I felt a glimmer of pride when I saw one of my mother's sculptures placed delicately on her desk. It was a small one, probably the only kind she could afford, a woman with a buddha-ish belly and grotesque face. Mama's signature style—ugly and pretty at the same time. *Wonder where I get it from.*

When Riley saw me looking at the sculpture, her face burned red with embarrassment. I wasn't sure why she felt ashamed, most people like my mother's work.

But, back to the puzzles.

When Riley said she liked doing puzzles, she forgot to mention that she also likes to *make* them. She had a large steel die-cutting machine and thousands of corrugated cardboard sheets and molds for making her own designs.

For the first time, I realized: *we never once asked Riley about her art.* She was always quiet as a mouse, timid even, often listening instead of contributing during our weekly lunch sessions. We all had our own things; for me, it was painting, obviously. Sammy had her whole digital and graphic design thing, and Scarlett ... well, Scarlett was Scarlett, putting a face to the art, and all that.

Riley's puzzle-making equipment took up her entire bedroom, and since the tiny 600-square-foot apartment housed *only* one bedroom, I couldn't help wondering where the girl slept. There wasn't a bed in sight.

Does she even sleep? I wondered, looking around at all the completed and half-done puzzles lying around on the floor. For the first time, I noticed how pale she was, purple half-moons shading her eyes, zombie-like. *But the puzzles are freaking brilliant.*

"So, I have an idea. Hear me out." Riley was usually quiet, but not tonight. Something lit from within as she stood by her shiny machine, stroking the steel like a prized family pet.

I liked her more than I ever had in that moment. That night, I saw something behind her eyes ... something that reflected my own. *Passion. The kind that gets down deep in your bones and leads to obsession.*

"Okay ... should we be scared?" Scarlett said. She looked distracted and slightly disgusted by the paltry apartment. In her arms, she was still carrying those cases of Corona with a bottle of Patron on top, and her pupils were tiny little pinpricks. She thought we didn't know about the drugs, but it was obvious to everyone who knew her.

"Yeah. Are you going to hack us up in your machine? Turn us into fleshy meat puzzles?" Sammy joked. She was poking at an all-black puzzle, nose scrunched.

I narrowed my eyes at my roommate. *That girl isn't right in the head. I love Sammy, but her sense of humor is a little off, most people missing her punchlines completely.*

"Ha! No, nothing like that," Riley said, strangely serious. "I was thinking we could come up with our own design together and then I'll make it into a puzzle. Afterwards, we can put it together. I might not have much room in here, but I do have a big kitchen table we can work at. Much better to put a puzzle together when you build it yourself…" She was rambling, obviously nervous.

"Whoa. That sounds fucking awesome," Scarlett said.

Riley's mouth spread into the biggest grin I'd ever seen.

I nodded. "Definitely."

Riley looked to Sammy last. She was always the skeptic, so I could see why Riley felt the need for her approval. As Sammy's roommate and oldest friend, I often caught myself tiptoeing around her, trying to keep her pleased, as well. On nights when she was working at the smoke shop, I felt more relaxed, more myself in the apartment alone.

Sammy shrugged. "Sure. I'm in. But I was thinking—"

"No. Don't you go trying to micro-manage this, Sammy," I warned, giving her a playful shove.

"No, no. Seriously. I'm not going to do that. I was just thinking … what if we used your design, Mia? The creepy painting of Monroe. Your painting, my digital skills, and Riley doing her thing on that crazy-ass chopping machine… How cool would that be?" Sammy suggested. There was something in the way she said it, something fiery behind the eyes. *Maybe we all have a little fire in us.*

I couldn't help feeling a little surprised that she wanted to use my Monroe design though. *Sammy loves me, I know that. But there's always this line between us, a thin veil separating friendship from competition.*

We grew up in the same town with the same friends … and for most of it, Sammy resented my popularity, but more than that, she resented my art. More than anything, I think she resented my advantage when it came time to apply for Monroe. I got a full ride—some would say it was because of my mom, but I liked to think I did it all on my own. And even after I got kicked out in freshman year, they let me come back. *Maybe it's a mixture. I can't deny I'm privileged; hell, I grew up with Cristal Ludlow as a mother.*

When *Monroe—Another View*, my painting, was displayed on campus and featured in several prominent magazines, Sammy barely batted an eye. It's not that she didn't notice; I think she was jealous. She only mentioned the painting a couple times; it was a sore spot for her, I think. Hearing her suggest it as our puzzle design now gave me hope that all those hard feelings of the past had finally slipped away...

"Sounds good to me. Or, you know, we could use one of your own original graphic designs instead, Sammy," I offered.

"No way. We should do yours. It's the best. What do you two think?" Sammy turned to look at Scarlett and Riley.

Scarlett shrugged. "Fine by me."

Riley was grinning ear to ear, cheeks blossoming with pleasure. I was relieved to see a little color on her translucent skin. "I would love that," she said, gleefully.

So, that's how it started.

I guess if someone were to blame for Alaska and all that transpired there, it was me. After all, it was my design on the puzzle that started this rocky little friendship of doom.

Chapter Three

Scarlett

L et's be real: I'm the least talented one in the group.

It's no secret, really. And honestly, I don't give a damn. But … that first night at Riley's apartment, I'd never felt more certain of it than I did right then: I was the odd one out of the four of us.

I didn't even know Riley made puzzles. I should have, considering I was the first one to make friends with the girl. Frankly, I was impressed. I didn't know how she could afford that equipment—*hell, where did the girl even sleep?*

Riley was painfully shy and withdrawn when I met her, but because of me, she was starting to come out of her shell. On that first day when I approached her in class, inviting her to join us for lunch, I was more than a little high, and more friendly than usual. I don't know why I befriended her. Maybe I was a little bored…

Truth is, though, I liked her. Riley was quiet and thoughtful, balancing out my boisterous side.

But with Mia's God-given painting abilities and Sammy's graphic art skills … and Riley's woodworking genius … where did that leave me in this equation?

Well, I'll tell you where—at the dead center, pulling the strings, as usual.

Because, the truth is, none of this ever would have lifted off the ground if it weren't for me.

When the design was done, I was the one who took the pictures. I was the one who presented the first finished puzzle to all of my fans online.

Because of me it went viral.

So, that's how it started.

I made a simple post—*look what me and my friends made!*

I added the proper hashtags of course, hoping for at least a thousand likes. Then we woke up to 300k likes and dozens of requests: *Where can I get one? How much? What's your Venmo? Do you do custom designs?*

The girls were humbled by the attention, but they didn't quite understand it.

Fame is a gift. You use it or lose it.

I pressured them. "We need to use this rise in popularity to our advantage. Feature ourselves all over the place online, force everyone to pay attention while we have them at our fingertips…"

"We should celebrate first … take a trip together," Riley suggested, shocking the hell out of me. She was always the quiet one, but I liked her more in that moment.

"We could focus on our art. I could make more puzzles for Scarlett to post... We could even join some of our designs and make plans on our little girls' retreat."

Sammy was the first to say no. She had work to consider, and she didn't want to leave her brother Rob even for a short trip.

Mia said, "I don't know..." but she didn't really offer any good reasons not to.

I loved the idea of a girls' trip, a chance to bond and work on our art. A chance to celebrate the end of summer. But mostly, I needed to get away from my own self … my own bad habits. If I ever wanted to be as talented as the other girls, I had to get my shit together.

It wasn't easy to change their minds. But influencing was *my* role.

I knew they'd come around sooner or later.

Chapter Four

Sammy

I might be the Debbie Downer of the group, but in truth, I'm the only one with sense, sometimes.

If there was one person who got this thing off the ground and kept it from floating away in the clouds … well, that was me. I was the one who got us the house in Alaska for the summer. And I even found it for free. Well, it was my brother that mentioned it … and it couldn't have come at a better time.

The idea of taking a girls' trip to focus on our art and celebrate our recent viral trip was a good one, but normally, I would have said no. Unlike the others, with their trust funds and scholarships, I had student loans out the wazoo. That's why I worked full time, barely sleeping as I ran back and forth between the smoke shop and class. But everything had changed now. School had come to an end, my future plans in limbo, and with issues at my current job, I didn't have that to rely on anymore either.

The availability of an exclusive island in Alaska couldn't have come at a better time.

I know numbers and maps, exactly what it will take—money and time-wise—to get there. Plus, I was the only one who didn't waste my time drinking and gabbing and working on frivolous paintings all day. They needed me to organize the trip, or else it would have just been a pipe dream, something we talked about while we were drunk and making puzzles.

They needed someone level-headed in charge. They needed *me*.

"What's the matter, Riley?" I asked, trying to hide my annoyance. She was too quiet, too timid. Something about that bothered the hell out of me.

"I'm fine, I promise," Riley said, but she obviously wasn't fine.

"Spit it out. What are you anxious about?"

"It's the whole Alaska thing," Riley said, eyes lifting to meet mine.

"What's wrong with Alaska?" I asked, pacing back and forth on the worn carpet in front of where the girls were curled up on mine and Mia's sofa.

Scarlett looked away guiltily, sipping on a full glass of Jägermeister.

"You too?" I asked, pointedly.

"It's just … I'm not fond of Alaska either," Scarlett admitted, slamming back the rest of the drink then wiping her mouth with a long black sleeve. "Isn't it cold there all the time? And dark half the time? Fuck that, Sammy. If we're going somewhere remote to focus on our art, can it at least be warm and tropical?"

"I'm a nervous flyer…" Riley blurted out, sheepishly.

Why does that not surprise me? I gave Mia a look that said, "Can you believe this girl?" but she looked away, patting Riley on the shoulder like a baby kitten.

"Yes, Scarlett, there *are* places in Alaska that go dark for long periods of time. It's because of the way the Earth is tilted… Well, never mind. The important thing here is that most of the state does not go dark, and even those parts that do are for only thirty to sixty days. It won't affect us where we're going. Also, Alaska isn't cold in the summer. It's like eighty degrees in some places!" I said.

Scarlett tilted her head side to side, considering, then reached for another drink.

"And as far as flying, Riley, we can get you a sedative. One of my foster dads used to be terrified of planes, but then the doctor gave him something to take for the flight on the way to Nevada. He slept like a baby the whole way there. Fear of flying is something you need to get over, anyway."

Riley nodded, but still, I could tell she wasn't on board.

"I don't get it. Why Alaska? We could go anywhere…" Mia started.

I felt a flash of annoyance. Mia was my best friend, but until the others had showed up to discuss this, she'd made no mention about any doubts. *She's supposed to be on my side.*

"Alaska wouldn't have been my first choice either," I sighed. "But after our talks the other night about focusing on our art, I figured this was the first place to disconnect. No one can reach us there. And my brother found it. It will be completely free for three whole months; all we have to do is pay for our flights and a boat ride to the island."

"Your brother. Really, Sammy? What does he have to do with any of this?" Mia said, bitterly.

Mia and my brother Rob didn't get along. They'd dated for a while and it hadn't ended well. Since Mia and I are roommates, I usually don't feel comfortable inviting him over to the apartment we share. And even when he calls, Mia acts like her feelings are hurt. As though I must choose her or my brother. *Ridiculous.*

"He's the reason I came up with Alaska. His friend sent him a picture of this, said we could stay there rent-free for three months. I repeat: rent-fucking-free."

I took the map out of my back jeans pocket and unfolded it. I spread it across the coffee table in front of them for all to see.

"This," I pointed at the map, "is Whisper Island."

It was a hand-drawn map. And although Mia liked to think of herself as the "real artist" in the group, I'm a pretty good sketch artist myself.

"Okay," Mia said, squinting at it then looking back up at

me, questioningly. "Are we hunting treasure or what?" she said, a ripple of laughter in her tone.

Ignoring her, I said, "The island is ten square miles, located near the tip of the Alaskan Peninsula. It is surrounded by the mysterious Bering Sea. It's one of the most beautiful places on earth."

The girls looked at each other, still unsure.

"And, like I said, we'd get to stay there for free for three months."

They still didn't look convinced. The cool map and the incomparable price tag—or lack thereof—clearly wasn't enough. *But I knew that before I brought it up. I couldn't tell them the truth—that going to a deserted island and getting the hell out of Tennessee was my best bet right now, with or without them.*

"Let me show you the real pictures of it," I said.

I crossed the room and retrieved my backpack. I'd printed out dozens of photos my brother had sent me online, using up every bit of high-resolution ink on my printer.

"This is Whisper Island," I repeated, dumping the glossy photos on the table in front of them.

I'm not sure which one of them gasped first, but I knew I had them then.

Whisper Island was breathtaking; an isolated strip of heaven with a miniature mansion and three workable outbuildings. *It's perfect for me*, I thought.

"All we would need is our plane tickets and we're on our way there…"

Of all the girls, Riley looked the most mesmerized, locking in on the photos. She held one up of the main house on the property, studying the shiny glass windows on the second floor as though she could see a tiny person inside.

"How soon can we go?" Riley asked, breathlessly.

So, that's how it started.

I took our little idea and simple plan and turned it into something real … but also something magical.

"This will be quite the adventure," Scarlett said, smiling with all her teeth.

I hope so, I thought, cringing internally.

The Voyage

Chapter Five

Riley

It's a fourteen-hour flight to Alaska.

I can't even fathom how it will feel to be stuck on this plane after four hours, much less fourteen.

"You should have taken it sooner," Scarlett scolded, referring to my prescription for Xanax the doctor gave me. The pill bottle was burning a hole in my right jeans pocket. The doctor had assured me that it was fast-acting and effective but might make me sleepy and uncoordinated.

As nervous as I was about the long flight, the thought of embarrassing myself in front of my new-ish friends seemed worse.

"I think I'll wait until take-off," I breathed, wriggling around in my narrow seat, hips already digging into the arm rests. The air in the cabin seemed to shrink by the minute.

Scarlett was crammed in the tiny seat beside me, wearing skinny jeans, a black hoodie, and flats. Her red hair smelled like cinnamon and cloves, and she was wearing it up today in a tight, high braid. A pair of sunglasses perched lazily on her head even though the sun wasn't up yet. As always, Scarlett's lips were blood red and gorgeous, matching the vibrant color of her hair. It looked brighter and redder than usual, and for the first time, I wondered if it was natural or dyed.

"All right, but don't say I didn't warn you … and don't go freaking out on me, Rye. I'm not your mama and I don't like getting barfed on."

"As though you get barfed on all the time." I tried to laugh but my voice sounded tinny and strange. *I can't believe I'm doing this. I can't believe I'm headed to Whisper Island.* My heartbeat fluttered like moths' wings in my chest. I'd told the girls it was my first time on a plane, but that was a lie, it was actually my fifth. Those first several times I had been filled with dread, unable to breathe for most of the flight.

Across the aisle, Sammy and Mia looked relaxed. Mia was wearing pajama pants and a ratty Monroe sweatshirt, black hair twisted in a knot on the top of her head. She had obviously rolled straight out of bed this morning, and who could blame her? It was only 6.30am now, so we'd had to meet and drive to the airport at 3.30 this morning.

Sammy was wearing her wireless ear buds. She looked comfortably uncomfortable in a pressed pair of khakis and a long-sleeved button-down blouse. She glanced over at me, glasses slipping down her nose, and gave me a snarky half-smile. "Don't freak out, Riley. We need you in Alaska," she yawned.

I tried to catch Mia's eye beside her, but she was staring at a book in her lap, motionless. She'd been on the same page since we'd boarded and it was obvious she wasn't really reading; she was busy giving the silent treatment to Sammy and, ultimately, the rest of us too.

I hope she settles down before we get to Alaska.

But I couldn't blame Mia for being upset. Not after what Sammy had sprung on us at the last minute.

Sammy's brother Rob was coming to Alaska, too, even though it was supposed to be only us four.

I'd never met Rob, but Scarlett—being the gossip queen she is—had filled me in late last night after leaving Sammy and Mia's apartment.

Rob was a few years older than Sammy, but you'd never know it based on the nature of their relationship. They'd lost their parents at a young age and Rob had struggled with drug and alcohol addiction since his early teens, most of the adult responsibilities falling to Sammy. Eventually, they'd gone into foster care, moving from one foster family to the next, sometimes together and sometimes not. After Rob's high school graduation, the siblings had lived together for a short time until Rob had run off to Toledo with a girl. According to Scarlett, Sammy had been a mess over it, worried to death for her "baby-not-so-baby brother".

I wasn't sure how Scarlett knew all this, exactly, considering that she'd only become friends with Sammy and Mia during their freshman year at Monroe. Sometimes, I got the sense that Scarlett liked to fill in her own details, making each story a little more sensational than the last. A born storyteller.

Shortly before applying to Monroe, Sammy ran into an old friend from high school—Mia. Mia had plans to go there too, so they decided to rent a cheap two-bedroom apartment in Memphis. Some weeks after they had moved, Rob had shown up on their doorstep, begging Sammy to forgive him and let him stay with her for a while.

That's how he and Mia ended up dating. And when it all fell apart between them because of Rob's philandering, Sammy was worried she'd lose them both. Her brother or her best friend, not an easy choice. She was determined to maintain her relationship with both, but she did it from afar. *Until now.*

"She'll be all right, just give her some time to be mad," Scarlett whispered, knocking her knee against mine. Mia looked positively sullen, quieter than I'd ever seen her. And she hadn't looked at Sammy once so far today.

I hope she gets past this.

None of us were happy about Rob coming. Mia had

responded so vehemently, there was no room left for Scarlett or me to speak up at that point.

Sammy had argued: "Jeez, Mia. You should be over it by now. It's been years since you all dated, and you know how much he means to me... He's trying to stay clean and sober and I need him with me. And he's the one that has the friend with the island, remember? So, it's not like I could say no."

But Mia didn't understand. She was furious he was coming.

Sammy's brother must have really hurt her when they split...

"Can't someone else take care of him? Or better yet, let him take care of himself! He's almost thirty, for Christ's sake!" Mia had whined.

"How could you ask me that? You know there's no one else, Mia. You know that better than anyone," Sammy had said.

Mia's face softened for the first time since learning the news. "Sorry. It's just not a good idea. Even if we didn't have history, I'd feel the same way. My feelings for him are long gone, trust me on that..."

"He'll stay out of the way, I promise," Sammy had replied.

So, it was agreed upon, even though none of us really agreed. Rob was coming too.

Sammy couldn't leave her vulnerable, self-destructive brother behind, and we had to stick it out and support her because she was our friend and because she was the one who had presented the location to us.

I didn't mind it. After all, the island was good-sized; there was enough room for everyone. The house itself had five bedrooms, not to mention all the extra outbuildings on the property too.

There's plenty of room to keep Mia and Rob apart.

Rob's job wouldn't let him off until Sunday, so we had a one-day head start on him anyhow. *Hopefully, by the time he reaches the island, Mia will have come to terms with the idea. Hopefully, she'll be so excited about our venture and so enamored with the island that she won't care,* I thought, smiling to myself.

There was a dull click and a sudden rush of static, then the pilot's voice filled the cabin. He announced that we were "cleared for takeoff". I felt my chest and throat constrict.

Hands rattling, I struggled to dig around in my too-tight pocket to retrieve the tiny orange bottle of pills. I'd been worried they'd take the medicine from me in security, but they hadn't.

The whole process of getting on the plane was so disorienting, plopping down in my seat had originally come as a huge relief.

But now the earth was moving underfoot, picking up speed...

"Let me help." Scarlett snatched the bottle from my hand and popped the cap.

She fished out an egg-shaped pill then offered me her water bottle. I tossed the tiny pill to the back of my throat and took a long swig of lukewarm water. I knew it couldn't work that quickly, yet I instantly felt calmer.

Scarlett grinned. "One for you. Three for me." Before I could stop her, she tapped three of the pills in her palm and swallowed them without water.

"Brace for impact," she said, grinning with all her teeth.

Chapter Six

Mia

I frowned at the side of my best friend's face. As usual, Sammy was makeup-free, her short brown hair combed neatly, but dull and boring. Sammy and I barely spoke this morning after the alarm went off, riding in silence to pick up the other girls for our early morning flight.

I'd expected her to at least apologize. *Why did she drop the Rob-bomb at the last second like that? It's almost like she wanted to stun me. She knows how I feel about her brother. How could she do this to me?*

I'd always known how close Sammy and Rob were; well, honestly, it was more like Sammy being overly involved and obsessed with her brother's life, while he didn't give a damn about her. *Sammy is such an enabler! I wonder if Rob ever asks her questions about her own life ... how she's doing... I wonder if Rob ever asks her about me.*

There was something so off about it. I knew Rob was living with friends in nearby Knoxville, delivering pizza out of his van for Spinelli's.

We didn't discuss Rob often—it was a touchy subject for me, and Sammy knew that, or at least I had thought she did —but still, last time she talked about him he was doing just fine. *Why now? Forty-eight hours before go-time? Why the sudden announcement that he was coming too? I'm amazed he could even find a flight as quickly as he did!*

It wasn't that I didn't trust Sammy's motives. She probably believed him when he said he needed her support and wanted to come... It was him I didn't trust. *What if Rob's running from the law and that's why he decided to invite himself to Alaska with us?*

The sort of trouble Rob could get into varied from any number of things... He'd once gotten locked up for driving a stolen car that he claimed he didn't know was stolen (Sammy believed him, of course), and of course, there were also the drugs. He had a hankering for opiates.

The last thing I need is trouble following me to Alaska. I agreed to go away so I could get away from the rumors circling again about my past. The past IS the past ... and I wanted to leave it there. Including my relationship with Rob.

As impulsive as Rob is, maybe he'll change his mind or miss his flight on Sunday, and then he'll never show up at all... Wouldn't that be ideal?

It was a terrible thought, and one I knew would only cause Sammy worry and pain, but I couldn't help wishing it for myself. Plain and simple: *Rob Mackey broke my fucking heart. Moving forward after graduation … I want to start somewhere new, letting my mistakes and heartaches fade behind me on my way out the door.*

The island had seemed like the perfect place to start with my three best friends, and Rob coming had brought the whole heavenly plan crashing down before my eyes…

For a while, like Sammy, I'd believed Rob's charm. I bought into the bullshit stories, trusted every word he said … and he left me feeling enchanted at a time when I needed someone—anyone—to believe in me and not just see the mistakes I made in freshman year.

But then—and there's always a "but then" with guys like Rob—I found out about the other girl. Excuse me —*girls*, plural.

Embarrassingly enough, I didn't leave it at that. *I forgave him. Not once, but several times.*

But alas, cheaters are always cheaters. *Isn't that what they always say?*

Wearily, I stared at my best friend, listening to the soft purrs of her snoring. *There's something she's not telling me about Rob, I just know it. I can feel it deep in my bones. This entire trip came so out of the blue, and Sammy is rarely spontaneous.*

Across the aisle, Scarlett and Riley were sleeping. Scarlett's bright red mouth was wide open, head tilted at an awkward angle. And Riley's head was slumped on Scarlett's shoulder.

At least the Xanax worked its magic on Riley, I thought, tiredly. I was also shocked that Scarlett had agreed to come. A fun trip was something that screamed Scarlett's name, but a trip to a remote island with no Instagram, Snapchat, or Twitter gossip...? Not really her thing. For the first time, I wondered if she, too, had her own reasons for coming. And Riley. She was the first to suggest it, despite her fear of flying... *Does she really know us well enough to go on a girls' trip this far away?*

For the first time since meeting Riley, I wondered if she, too, knew about the skeletons in my freshman closet.

It was still early, but I lifted the window shade an inch. Bright morning sun filtered through, and I felt Sammy stir beside me.

"Damn you, Mia. That's too bright," Sammy muttered sleepily, pushing her glasses around on her face.

I slid the shade all the way up, letting the sun stream through. *I can't believe Sammy ruined everything by inviting her stupid brother. I could kill her for putting me in this position.*

"Serves you right, Sammy," I said, staring out at the puzzle-piece squares of farmland below.

Chapter Seven

Scarlett

Although my legs had turned to Jell-O and my butt felt flatter than usual, I was wide awake and grinning as I rolled my luggage through the double glass doors of the airport.

"Ah. Fresh Alaskan air!" I cheered, stopping to allow my friends to catch up.

Mia and Sammy were dragging, zombie-like, fighting to stay awake. For the life of me, I couldn't figure out why they didn't sleep on the plane. I, for one, had taken advantage of the long flight and slept for most of it.

Riley had slept some too, and like me, she looked excited to reach Alaska.

"Wow. Look," Riley gushed, rolling up her bag beside mine. She pointed. The road outside the terminal was scattered with cars, but beyond that, white-blue mountains glowed in the distance. Despite the 60-degree weather (which actually felt more like 40 or 50 degrees, to me) the mountains were still capped with tiny white brushes of snow.

"It's pretty here, but I'm sure we'll see more once the driver gets us out of here," I said, smiling.

"It's cold as fuck out and I'm exhausted," Mia moaned, sitting her backpack and suitcase on the curb then plopping down beside them. "Where is our driver? You did stick with *that* plan, right?" she snapped at Sammy.

Guess she's still bitter about Rob coming, I thought, with a smirk.

I'd never admit it to the others, but I wasn't completely opposed to Sammy's brother joining us on the island. Sure, he was kind of an asshole, but he was sexy in that bad boy, hate-to-love-him sort of way, and … a little drama on the island might help with the boredom, right? Sammy had mentioned that Rob was also trying to stay clean and sober. The thought of having someone else on the island who could relate with my issues gave me a strange tingling sensation in my belly.

Truth was that the idea of coming here wasn't one I was crazy about at first. Staying on a tiny island with no cell service, not to mention Wi-Fi, was not my idea of a good time. But I couldn't let my friends leave me behind, not after our recent excitement with the viral post. And the more I thought about it … the more I knew getting away was the best thing for my sobriety. I'd had too many close calls recently, although I'd never admit that to the others.

I'd snort a few pills, then forget what I'd taken and take more... My stepmom had recently found me nearly unconscious after taking too many... She and my dad hadn't cut me off yet, but they'd made veiled threats that made me wonder if that day was coming soon...

I imagined myself on the island, snapping gorgeous photos ... and instead of worrying about uploading them right away and choosing the perfect hashtag, as usual, I'd be forced to take my time and really sift through the pictures, searching for internet gold. Searching for myself, with a clear head for once.

My friends think my area of expertise is partying and gossiping and posting selfies on Instagram, but in reality ... photography is my jam. I like seeing life in pictures, one flash of memory at a time...

Every single picture tells a story. And stories are what I love...

"The driver is coming. He should be here in the next few minutes," Sammy grumbled and narrowed her eyes at Mia.

I hope they're not at each other's throats the entire trip. And what will happen when Rob arrives on Sunday?... Will it get worse between the pair?

"Well, I hope the driver hurries," Mia said, chewing on the tips of her fingers as she waited.

I stole a glance over at Riley. Her eyes were still zeroed in on those mountains in the distance. *Hypnotized.*

"Xanax still working, is it?" I teased. Riley gave me a weary look, probably remembering that I had stolen three.

I probably shouldn't have done that. But I'd needed something to take the edge off and since we hadn't technically arrived at the island yet, it had felt okay to cheat on my new drug-free diet.

"Well, at least we made it. We're here," Sammy said. She left Mia sulking on her suitcase and came over to stand next to Riley and me. "Now all we need to do is get a good night's rest and tomorrow we'll take a boat to the island…"

"Yeah. Sounds like fun," I said, dully. My good mood was starting to evaporate, as I thought about taking a few more Xanax. *I wonder if they're still in her pocket. Would she give me one if I asked?*

Nononono.

"Hey, it's still pretty early, guys. We should go out for dinner and drinks before we check in to the motel. Celebrate our first night here…" I suggested. The thought of lying around in a hotel room, completely clean and sober, waiting for our boat ride tomorrow, seemed unbearable.

Alaska was four hours ahead of our time zone; it wasn't a huge difference, but it would take some getting used to.

"No way. I'm too tired," Sammy grumbled.

And Mia's too grumpy, I wanted to add but didn't.

"Maybe we could order some pizza, take showers, and if we're not too tired … run through our plans for tomorrow," Riley suggested, cheerily. The more I got to know the girl, the more she reminded me of a mouse. She always seemed so quiet and secretive, not to mention timid. But when she was excited, she turned perky and silly. Considering how different our personalities were, it annoyed me slightly. And the thought of pizza and soda was boring.

Before I could answer, a green Toyota 4Runner pulled up to park at the curb.

The passenger window came rolling down, revealing a young, hot driver. He had thick black hair and sunglasses. When he removed his shades, I was stunned by his gold-green eyes. *Wow. Maybe this ride won't be so boring after all*, I thought.

"I'm here for transport to Molly's. You Scarlett Schreiber?"

I smoothed my long red braid with one hand, gripping the handle of my suitcase with the other. "The one and the only," I said with a smile.

Chapter Eight

Sammy

Molly's Motel was exactly how I had pictured it in my mind when I'd booked a room for 60 bucks per night. It was drab and dreary, a lonely flat gray slab out in the middle of nowhere. Blinking vacancy sign with "cable TV!" written below. *Dull. But then again, this is our second-to-last leg of the voyage and then we'll be there on the island. Safe and sound.*

I was sure that there were nicer places with nicer views, but considering we only needed it for one night, to sleep and prepare for the boat ride out to the island tomorrow, it hadn't seemed worth spending more of our budget than necessary.

"This place is a shithole," Mia complained.

I bounced up and down on the bed, springs groaning, and ignored her.

Yes, she's still pissed that Rob's coming. But it's not like I had much of a choice in the matter. And her bad attitude is exhausting!

The beds were small, barely full size, with thin, moth-eaten blankets and a tiny TV set that looked like it came from my parents' living room in the Eighties. *At least they have "cable TV!"*, I thought, drearily.

"Here's our pizza." Riley opened the greasy cardboard box from Rosa's—the only pizza place around for miles—and took a whiff. "Come get some, guys," she said.

She was being overly cheerful, trying to lift mine and Mia's moods. Mia hadn't slept on the plane at all, which didn't surprise me. She had enough problems sleeping at home, in our apartment, often having nightmares and lucid dreams.

She'd made a point of keeping me awake on the flight here, opening her window or bumping me with the book she was reading any time I tried to nod off. It seemed childish, not to mention rude—*Rob is my brother. She has to understand that family comes first.*

Mia is an only child. Maybe that's why she doesn't understand?

We took turns loading up our paper plates with sausage and mushroom pizza. I half-expected Mia to start complaining about the mushrooms, but she sat on the edge of our bed, chewing mutely.

"So, tomorrow..." Scarlett said, looking around the room at us, one at a time. She was jittery and agitated, and for a moment, I wondered if she needed a drink of something or a toke. *She can't be that hooked, can she?*

"Is everyone excited?" Scarlett asked, stabbing at her pizza with a plastic fork but not eating.

"I am," Riley perked up. *Something about her over-eager-beaver attitude was getting under my skin. Something about it felt too fake, too try-hard, for my liking.*

I swallowed a bite of pizza and cleared my throat. "Juan and his crew are meeting us here at 9am. They'll take us to the dock, and he'll transport us to Whisper Island from there."

"Not Daniel picking us up again? Too bad." Scarlett frowned. I couldn't help it; I rolled my eyes. She'd flirted with our driver, Daniel, the whole way, from the airport to the motel. Nobody else could get a word in edgewise, not that Mia or I were in the mood for talking anyway. To make it worse, she'd given him her cell phone number when he dropped us off, even though we'd be out of range for months, besides our occasional trips for supplies on the mainland.

"Yeah, too bad it's not Daniel," I said, evenly. "So, as I was saying ... Juan is meeting us in the morning. The adventure begins soon."

"I can't wait," Riley chimed in.

Scarlett wasn't listening. She had her face in her phone,

texting with both thumbs furiously. *Already chatting with that driver, probably.*

She's in for a rude awakening when she has to learn to get by on the island with no phone and no internet.

"I'm going to bed," Mia said, abruptly. She got up and tossed her half-eaten pizza in the small garbage can, then plopped down on the bed. She stretched out and rolled over on her right side, facing the wall.

I could feel her anger and sadness pulsating from across the room.

"Mia. Can we talk?" I asked. She made a sound, a cross between a sigh and a grunt, back still turned to me.

"Let's go see if we can find a soda machine in this place," Scarlett suggested to Riley. Moments later, they were both slipping out of the room, giving me apologetic, knowing looks.

At that moment, I was grateful for their understanding. *Mia and I are so close. We can't go to Whisper Island fighting like this…*

"You're like a sister to me, you know that?"

"Uh huh. Sure," Mia grumbled.

She was being childish, still turned away from me. But for once, I chose to overlook it.

"I'm sorry about Rob. Truly, I am."

"If you were sorry, then you wouldn't have invited him in the first place. What happened to this being a girls' trip … focusing on our art and all that other bullshit you said? And…"

"And what?" I pressed.

"And you know how much I fucking cried." As soon as the words were out of Mia's mouth, I could hear the shaky tears in her voice, fighting to burst from within at any moment. I felt a stab of guilt in my chest. *She cried for a long time over my brother. I do know that.*

"He really hurt you, I know... My brother can be an asshole. I know that better than anyone," I said.

"Then why? Can you at least tell me that? Because I've known you long enough to know when you're hiding something from me. You've been weird lately, Sammy. And this shit with Rob, out of the blue like this... Something's not right, is all," Mia said.

She turned to me, eyes wide open and concerned, arms tucked in close to her chest, protective. She had also been acting weird lately, but this didn't seem like the right time to bring it up.

I wasn't planning on telling her the truth, but then my lips were moving ... words falling out too fast...

"I had no other choice. It's not his fault this time, okay? This time it's mine," I said, breathily.

Mia sat up, eyes scrunched up in confusion. "What the hell does that mean, Sammy? Out with it."

I took a deep breath. "Okay. Listen. It wasn't safe in Memphis. That's why I agreed to come. That's why I jumped at Rob's friend's offer to come here ... so far away, so secluded... I got myself in some trouble, Mia. I had no choice but to leave when I did. Please believe me." My body was tight with tension and fear as the words spilled over.

"What is it? What did Rob do?" Mia asked, eyes wide.

Shaking my head back and forth, I said, "It's not Rob, don't you see? I'm the one who fucked up this time. If I'd left him behind, he might have been in danger too. I'd never forgive myself if something happened to my brother..."

The Island

Chapter Nine

Riley

My face and belly were burning, the water choppy as the wind blew viciously across my cheeks.

"You okay?" Scarlett asked, edging closer to me on the seat. She was wearing a thick green hoodie pulled up around her face, and without her bright red hair showing, she looked small and pixie-like.

I shivered. The sense of being so far out, stranded so far from land, no going back now ... was unsettling to say the least. The farther we got from the mainland, the more I couldn't shake the feeling of unease and impending doom. Here we were, open water on all sides ... and instead of feeling free, out in the open, walls were closing in around me, the claustrophobic sense of being stuck becoming unbearable. *There's no going back now.*

"I'm fine," I lied. "You?" My teeth knocked together uncontrollably.

"Great," Scarlett said, also chattering. Last night, she seemed bubbly and talkative, as usual, but today her skin had a ghostly tinge to it, her pallor and demeanor off. *Was it possible that I wasn't the only one nervous about this trip to the island?*

I thought about the way Scarlett gulped down those pills on the plane, greedy and desperate. *Perhaps she's coming off the effects of taking too many sedatives...*

Sammy and Mia were pushed together tightly, a narrow sliver of sunlight breaking between them. From here, they almost looked ... celestial.

Sammy's mouth was puckered, finger pointing ahead. Mia's head turned in the same direction.

I followed their gaze, trying to see what they were seeing, but a dense blanket of fog wrapped around the boat like a thick winter jacket.

I don't know what I imagined ... not this. *I pictured blue seas, calm water, clear all the way to the bottom ... and the island itself floating above like a fluffy green cloud...*

But the waters today were anything but calm, the boat rocking side to side, our suitcases and supplies throttling against the sides with each queasy wave, my stomach doing somersaults in tandem.

Water sloshed over the bow, threatening to overtake us. *How long it's been since I've been on water... This isn't how I expected it to feel.*

Juan drove the speedboat fast and carelessly, like he'd done it a million times.

"Right there! Don't you see it?" Sammy gushed to Mia, holding out her hand again. Mia, like me, was squinting, trying to catch a glimpse of Whisper Island.

Whisper Island—a place for ghosts.

Scarlett stiffened in the seat beside me.

"Look. There it is," her words like tiny little whispers through the fog.

I shivered, my whole body experiencing an unexpected shudder of … *what?* Fear? Anticipation? I wasn't sure anymore.

That's when I saw it: a thick tangle of trees, and knots of branches. They reached out from the water, like outstretched bony hands. *Beckoning me to the island.*

"My God. There it is…" It took me a moment to realize it was my lips moving … but the rush of wind blew my words back in my face. I looked at the others. They were all staring, mesmerized, not just by the island, but by the hulking shape in the middle—the house they'd seen in the pictures.

Just like that, the boat split through the fog like a hot knife in butter. As we grew nearer to our destination, the wind died down, the air becoming deadly silent around us, a cocoon of darkness.

Juan had eased off the gas, drifting jerkily toward the shore. My belly rocked with the boat, twisting and turning.

I couldn't take my eyes off the house. It was set back

from the trees, a tall gray ghost in the distance. It looked like the picture online, only ... older, more weatherworn and rundown. There was nothing luxurious about it; it looked positively eerie from where it sat.

I rubbed my eyes so I could see more clearly, my vision still spotty from the soot-colored fog.

"It looks like it's falling apart," Scarlett said, squirming in the seat beside me. She was scratching at her hands and wrists, clearly anxious. More anxious than I'd ever seen her.

But, strangely, she looked far from disappointed; in fact, a tiny smile was blooming, her cheeks pink with pleasure as she scratched and ogled the island.

"It's spooky but in a cool, gothic way, right?" Scarlett's lips tickled my ear lobe.

"Right you are," I said, mechanically. The boat approached a rotted old dock at the shore. There was an old john boat that looked older than the dock parked beside it, a small motor attached to the back. *That will be our only source of transportation for the next three months*, I thought. *I hope it doesn't have holes, and the motor runs...*

"Hang tight," Juan warned, getting to his feet. George and Frank, his helpers we'd met at the dock, leaned over the side of the boat, securing thick ropes as Juan guided it perfectly on the opposite side of the john boat.

My legs were shaky as I tried to stand, my whole body quivering as though my blood sugar were low. For the life of me, I couldn't remember the last time I'd eaten. *Oh yeah. That slice of slimy pizza at the hotel last night.*

"Easy now. One at a time," Frank said, stepping up to the dock and holding out a hand to Sammy.

"I'm fine, thanks," Sammy snapped, lifting herself out. She stepped onto the dock, adjusted the straps of her backpack on her shoulders, and shaded her eyes as she glared at the ugly old house.

I was trying not to look, hoping that if I blinked a few times it would evaporate and reappear as the nice, luxurious house from the pictures.

You should have known it would be abandoned and unkempt, a voice inside me scolded.

Mia let Frank help her out next, and Scarlett was soon to follow. She held her hand out as though she were waiting for Frank to kiss it. I nudged her backside, ready to get the hell out of the boat. My stomach still twisting and stretching even though we weren't moving anymore.

"Thank you," I said to Frank, taking his hand and stepping onto the dock with my friends. I hoisted my heavy pack up higher on my shoulders, then released a heavy sigh. *We made it. Now it's time. For good times, good friends … and my own personal demons to conquer*, I thought, drearily.

The three girls were looking out at the water as though they wanted to go back. But I stared up at the ragged old monstrosity looming before me. *Blink. Blink. Nope, it's still dilapidated and disfigured. Not nearly as nice as the photos…*

And for the next few months, this is where we'll call home.

Chapter Ten

Mia

"Charming," I mumbled to myself.

As we helped the men unload the suitcases on the dock, sweaty and puffing, I couldn't help feeling a cloud of disappointment—not only from me, but from everyone.

When the three men were out of earshot, I said to Riley, "We'll have to go back inland in a day or two, taking several trips, just to get supplies to fix this place up. How can we stay here when we're not even sure if the roof over our heads will cave in?" I pointed at the bowed ceiling and the rotting beams of one of the outdoor storage buildings.

The building had long been abandoned; there was nothing but concrete flooring and a few work benches to work on. I'd imagined myself sneaking away from the others, doing some art on the island, getting a little me-time in one of the outbuildings. But the outdoor spaces looked as worn as the big ugly house itself.

"It's not quite what I imagined either." Riley spoke softly.

Sammy sighed. "Look, guys. We got this place for the next few months, and shall I remind you that's it free of charge? You can't beat free. We're going to have fun and focus on our art. We need this break, and it doesn't have to be fancy or glamorous for us to enjoy ourselves…"

But the more Sammy said that, the more it sounded like she was trying to deceive herself. Sammy had all but admitted last night that she was running from her problems back home. *I guess she could technically say the same about me…*

"Did you know it was like this?" Scarlett asked.

"Know what?" Sammy snapped. "That it was way more rundown than my brother said? Hell no! Of course, I didn't. I know it's not the Ritz Carlton, or the kind of place you pose in for your stupid Snap stories…"

I put up a hand. "Seriously, guys. Let's all take a deep breath. We haven't even been inside the house yet. And yeah, the island's overgrown and a little more secluded than we thought, but we'll still enjoy ourselves, won't we? We're surrounded by all this water and foliage…" *Now who's trying to convince herself?* I cringed internally.

I looked at each of my friends, giving them my best impression of a confident leader. I thought about the alternative: catching a plane back home. We had left town just in time to avoid the papers—the anniversary—and a news article with my name on it was probably headline news today back home. *Mia Ludlow, spoiled rich bitch, gets away with murder…*

I shuddered at the thought of going back now. *No, this place will suit just fine,* I thought, taking in the spindly branches stretching all around me.

"It's kind of cool, actually," Scarlett piped up. Despite being off the chilly water, her teeth were clicking together noisily. "It puts off spooky, gothic vibes. Kind of like your paintings, Mia."

I couldn't help it; I beamed. *Even now, I never grow tired of hearing praise for my work, even if it's coming from my friends who kind of have to say that shit. And even if I don't deserve anyone's praise after my past…*

"No internet. No phones. Most importantly, no distractions," I said. "We are going to create some amazing fucking art out here; I just know it."

Sammy was chewing on her lip, staring down at her feet. I remembered our strange conversation last night. *Was she serious about being in danger, or was she trying to make up excuses for inviting Rob along?*

When I agreed to come to Whisper Island, I wanted to get away to somewhere so far, even my spoiled reputation couldn't follow. I'd never once considered that Sammy had her own reasons, until she stunned me with her admission last night.

Sammy had sounded so certain, so scared for her life …

and when I woke up this morning, I was kind of hoping that it had all been a bad dream. That my best friend wasn't in danger. That coming here wasn't part of the plan because she was afraid to be home in Tennessee.

I tried to catch her eye, but she looked distracted. As though she could sense my thoughts, she lunged for the door, shouting after the men, "Oh, wait! Don't forget about picking up my brother tomorrow! He is supposed to call you when he's ready!" She disappeared through the heavy wood doors of the outbuilding, chasing after them.

I smiled sheepishly at Scarlett and Riley. Sammy and I were the closest, obviously, considering we'd been friends for so long, and roommates for the past two years. And I knew Scarlett pretty well; we'd been close since freshman year. But Riley was new to the group. She didn't know much about Rob, or how much him coming bothered me. *I guess that's one piece of my past I can't escape on Whisper Island...*

"You okay with Rob coming?" Riley asked, giving me a worried look.

My tough act melted away, my shoulders slumping. "Not really, but I'll have to be. He's Sammy's brother and it's not like I'd spend a vacation worrying about a guy anyway..."

"Fucking right," Scarlett said, squeezing my shoulder as she brushed past us and out the door, following Sammy.

Now it was just me and the new girl.

"This place isn't that bad, is it? A little crumbled and

creepy ... but maybe that's exactly what we need for a little inspiration. You can make some puzzles using your die casts and I'll create some kickass paintings," I said, thoughtfully.

"This place sort of reminds me of your painting where you show the dark side of the light. This is the flip side of what we expected, based on the pics we saw online. Not a bright, sunny island but a gloomy one, one with a history and secrets..."

How the hell would she know if this island had secrets? I wondered. But I liked her take on it—and she was right, it sort of *was* like the distorted version of perceived reality, like my paintings. *Like my entire life.* The good and bad, the past and the future ... *the terrible side of Mia.*

"Maybe it's meant to be that we came here," Riley said.

"Maybe so," I said, ruefully.

Chapter Eleven

Scarlett

I have to admit — *I'm sort of in love with Whisper Island.*

Maybe it's the way the wind whispers through the trees, taking its secrets all the way out to sea and back ... or maybe it's just the isolation and quiet. For the first time in a long time, I feel more like myself. *My real self.*

Not the me who spends hours choreographing funny skits on TikTok, or taking pics of my face from the right angle all while applying the most flattering filter, then sitting around and waiting for likes and comments, as though my entire self-worth depends on them.

No, out here ... there's no one to judge me. No way they can reach me either. And I can't reach out to people I don't need to talk to either. I have no choice but to let go of the vices I never should have developed in the first place.

I'm alone here safe from others, but, most importantly, safe from myself. Sure, I have my best friends with me, but they've always been my safety net — the place where I know I'll be on my best behavior.

Although I wasn't getting any cell service, I was glad to have my phone. I got the latest upgrade before we left, ensuring I could snap some fabulous pics while here. *For once, I'm not worried about what anyone thinks. I want to see the island through my own lens, view this space for my own pleasure, no one else's.* I lifted my phone and clicked the camera app, snapping several photos of the first outbuilding and walking over to the side of the house. The other girls had gone to wish the men goodbye, so I took the opportunity to wander.

Behind the main house, the woods grew thicker, but there was a narrow footpath that looked fairly new. As I followed it, visible among the nettles and thickets was another broken-down building. The vegetation was so overgrown, it almost looked like it was a part of the brambles, not the other way around.

Mesmerized, I ventured farther down the path, swatting branches and brush aside to get there.

There were three outdoor buildings on the property, according to the map, besides the main house. The first one, which was the one we'd already been inside, was empty and useless. I don't know what I'd been hoping for — perhaps a hot tub or jacuzzi outside?

I shook my head and laughed at myself. *If it sounds too*

good to be true it probably is. But Sammy is right: free is free. And hopefully, coming to Whisper Island, will help set me free from the drugs soon too.

The highs and the lows, the in-betweens ... I wanted to put all that behind me. I had no sources out here—no one to call and ask if they had anything to get me high today.

This must be the second building we saw on the map, I realized, as I reached it. It was less of an outdoor space and more like a little cottage. *Perhaps this is where the groundskeeper or waitstaff once stayed?* I wondered.

According to Sammy, the property once belonged to a family who hit hard times and had to leave Alaska. The property had never sold, which was hard to believe. *Even being so rundown, the island itself must be worth a fortune.*

I walked around the tiny building, searching for an entrance. Finally, on the backside, I spied a door. *How strange that's there no door on the frontside, facing the main property. Almost like whoever built it didn't want to see the water.* Vines and debris were blocking the door. Compelled to get inside, I started tearing away at the thick greens, trying to claw my way in ... then finally, with a solid push, the door creaked open.

Dust motes shivered in the shaft of light as I shimmied my way through.

Immediately, I realized I was right: this was some sort of guest house, not an extra storage building like we assumed while examining the map.

It was small, less than eight hundred square feet. A

lumpy brown mattress was pushed against the wall in the far-right corner, a stack of dusty old books on the bare wooden floor beside it.

Slowly, I moved through the room. My nose tickled with dust.

Who lived out here? I wondered. *Some sort of housekeeper?*

The bare-bones bed and single dresser were the only furniture in the room.

As much as my friends liked to tease me for my obsession with social media, most of my free time was spent reading books. I'd packed light for the trip since we were already so overloaded to begin with; some extra books to add to my reading stash sounded sublime. *When the withdrawals set in, I'd need to stay as occupied as possible to keep my mind off things while on the island...*

Intrigued, I crept over to the stack, plucking up the first book I saw. It was paperbound, the cover missing, and I could smell traces of smoke on its pages.

As I tried to flip through the pages, a few broke apart like dust in my hands.

That's a damn shame.

Setting the first book aside on the bed, I picked up the next one in the stack. It was leather bound and obviously some sort of journal or notebook. Curious, I flipped it open to the first page. There were only two lines on it, but I could see many more words on the pages beneath, the loopy impeccable handwriting bleeding through.

I zeroed in on the words. Two sentences, simple yet strange:

Elena Blackwater was the first to die. Many more will follow.

My breath lodged in my throat.

"Scarlett! Where are you?" I jumped and nearly dropped the book as I heard shouts coming from the footpath out front.

But instead of answering, I kept turning pages, ignoring the voice of my friend. *What has come over me?*

"There you are! Thank God," Sammy breathed, trying to squeeze through the wedged front door. She was bent at the waist, resting her hands on her knees. "We were worried. The guys just left. We have the island all to ourselves now. Ready to explore the main house?"

I nodded, solemnly. As Sammy scurried back through the door, I slipped the journal in the back of my jeans and tugged my sweater down to hide it. *There's no reason to spook them with this yet.*

Chapter Twelve

Sammy

There's something eerie about Whisper Island. Something looming and predatory. *But what did I expect from a place called "Whisper Island"?*

When Rob's friend Manny mentioned this place, I jumped at the idea. *You can't beat free, right? Plus, it was the perfect place to get away at a time when I needed it most.*

Getting the hell out of Tennessee was my number one priority.

"You're acting weird. Feeling all right?" I asked Scarlett, as we walked toward the other two girls waiting at the front of the main house.

"Yeah, of course. Just exhausted from the trip to get here and … cold." She looked pale, and despite being off the boat for nearly half an hour now, she still appeared to be freezing.

It was supposed to be 50 degrees, but the sun was settling low behind bulgy-black clouds, and I couldn't help wondering if a storm was approaching.

Water sloshed over the banks of the island, hungry and reaching. I tried not to think about what would happen if the water ever reached the house...

"Took y'all long enough," Mia teased as we joined them.

She was resting her suitcase on the ground by her feet, hair a mess as usual, her cheeks doughy and bright. After the whole Rob thing and our talk at the hotel last night, I'd half-expected her to turn around and go home. *But she's here, and she doesn't seem upset anymore. For now, at least.*

I glanced up at the house. The ground floor had a few bay windows, one of them cracked. Wind whistled through it noisily. The second story matched the first. More dark, cracked windows up top. It was built of gray bricks, which seemed fitting considering the current color of the water and sky.

Who lived here before? I wondered. Rob's buddy said they were distant relatives of his; that they'd left the island suddenly, and no one in the family wanted to claim it as their own afterwards. They tried to rent it out as much as possible, but the season had been slow with the coronavirus outbreaks.

An isolated place like this ... although normally inviting, I could see why it wasn't top choice for someone's dream vacation destination.

It was obvious that they hadn't done any renovations or

repairs in years. *Imagine paying to come here for a vacation, only to find out it's falling apart, the windows broken as though by vandals. Free is the only way to sell vacationers on it, at this point...*

I was starting to think maybe Rob's friend was lying about renting it out. There was no way they could get away with charging people to stay here. But for now, I was grateful he'd offered us the spot for a little while. I'd needed to get away... *The space between here and home is vast, and that's exactly what I need.*

Artists don't need fancy digs, right? In fact, many of the greats worked in squalor. Or at least, I thought so, perhaps reading that bit somewhere... This place is the perfect getaway, from your troubles and for fun...

The front porch sagged in the middle. As I climbed the steps, I prayed my weight didn't cause the wood to crack away and splinter, sucking my body down into the earth and hideous black seawater below.

"Did you check out the other buildings?" Riley asked.

"Yeah. Well, one—it was small. Probably not big enough to use for an art space or hangout. It's like a little guesthouse cottage," I said.

Riley nodded, staring nervously at the house. I wouldn't swear to it, but it almost seemed like she was holding her breath, waiting for me to go in first.

"What was in the other building?" I overhead Riley asking Scarlett.

"Nothing at all," Scarlett said, a defensive tone to her

voice. I shot her a funny look. *What is her deal?* For a moment, I wondered if something might be going on between her and Riley. *Maybe I've been so caught up in my own little tiff with Mia that I didn't consider what was going on with the others too.*

"Are you all ready?" I said. The welcome mat on the front porch was so dirty and rotten, I half expected it to fall apart in my hands as I lifted it. I produced a shiny gold key and held it up to show the others.

They joined me, finally edging up the steps. We stood side by side on the dumpy, sinking front porch. My friends looked leery, as though they wanted me to be the first to test it out.

"Come on, guys. I know it's rundown, but still: it's ours for the next few months. Those pictures Manny sent … well, I'm guessing they were at least a decade old, probably taken when this place was nicer and cleaner. But we'll fix it up, make it our own little summer retreat…"

Mia gave me a crooked smile. "Well, get on with it then."

I turned the key in the lock, and we stepped inside.

Chapter Thirteen

Riley

My first thought when we stepped inside was: *what a dump*.

But, when you looked past the grimy wood floors and the cobwebs in the corners, the place had a lot of old charm. The large living room had high ceilings and lacy white crown molding. The best part was the fireplace. It was adorned with green marble decorative tiles and appeared to be functional at first glance.

Black-and-white photographs were arranged on the mantelpiece.

Sammy started tugging white sheets off the furniture. "Ta-da!" She revealed a spotless leather armchair and sofa, then promptly sneezed.

She gave me a lopsided grin, as though she were saying, "Not so bad, eh?" as we eyed the furniture.

Not so bad at all, I thought, spinning around the room as I took in the full magnitude of the place. Sure, it needed some dusting and repairs, but it looked neat enough. I wasn't as disappointed as the others, feeling right at home in this dusty, cramped space.

"I'm going to check out the other rooms," Sammy said. Mia was already ahead of her, shouting for us to "Come and see how big this kitchen is! It looks like my great-grandma's china in the cupboards!"

Scarlett, on the other hand, stood motionless by the mantel, studying the photos closely. One picture was of a woman and two young girls, standing arm in arm. Their hair swayed in the breeze, sun glossy on their rose-red cheeks.

"Who do you think they were?" Scarlett breathed. I shrugged as I made my way down a long corridor that led to a tall, winding staircase.

"This isn't the kind of house you expect to find on an island. It's almost like they picked it up from some luxurious town in the Victorian era and dropped it here from the sky," Scarlett shouted after me.

It was a strange thing to say, an eerie thought, a weathered old house being dropped by a crane from the sky. I snaked my way up the stairs.

The others were still downstairs, and I wanted to take the opportunity to inspect the rooms. *Hopefully move into the biggest bedroom,* I thought, guilefully. There was one bedroom on the first floor and another four upstairs.

The upstairs landing opened into a long hallway, flanked by several closed doors on each side. I turned the cold brass knob of the first door, excitedly. There was something fun about being here; a life forgotten, another world so far away from civilization out here at sea...

As I opened the door, I came face to face with a man— beady black eyes, his mouth gaped open in surprise. I released an ear-splitting scream.

Chapter Fourteen

Mia

I was admiring the double Dutch ovens and wondering: *how in the hell did they get all these incredible appliances to the island? And why would someone leave this behind?* —when I heard the screams.

Sammy and I looked at each other, eyes widening in horror.

"Riley," we both said in unison, running through the corridor and following the sound of her shrieks upstairs. Scarlett was at our heels.

I reached the top of the stairs first. Immediately, I saw Riley in the corridor, gasping for air. Two people, a man and a woman, were standing in the hallway with sheepish grins on their faces.

All my fears evaporated, replaced with a feeling I knew too well: *pure, unadulterated rage.*

"What the fuck are you doing here, Rob?" I yelled.

Chapter Fifteen

Scarlett

I must admit I've always loved a good scandal.

Not only was Sammy's brother, and Mia's ex-lover, already on the island—*surprise!*—but he'd brought a guest along with him (*double surprise!*).

Mia's anger was palpable. It penetrated the walls, even though we couldn't see her.

She was in the kitchen, banging around with pots and pans. Opening tins of tomatoes and beans she'd packed for our first-night pot of chili.

Sammy didn't look happy with her brother either.

All of us—minus Mia—were piled in the living room, sitting on the dusty sofa and chairs.

"Why didn't you tell me you were coming early?" Sammy said.

Immediately, I noticed that her tone was different with Rob. If it were one of us who had surprised her, she'd be scolding us and dripping with sarcastic retorts by now.

Rob smiled guiltily and looked over at the girl on the couch beside him. She was a pretty girl, in that knife-to-your-heart sort of way. Skin, smooth and glossy. Thick auburn hair combed perfectly around her face. She was petite, with glossy pink toes on her sandaled feet. I noticed a skull tattoo on her left foot that looked out of place on her cutesy, elfin body.

"Truthfully? I didn't want you to get mad, sis. We got here a couple days early. We wanted to enjoy ourselves a little bit before everyone showed up, and Spinelli's let me off work to come after all."

"You wanted to enjoy yourself," Sammy said, drily. She looked from Rob to the girl again, waiting for him to introduce her.

I'd only seen Rob once from a distance when he dropped off something to Sammy at school. Of course, I'd kept up with his social media pages, as well. He was cuter in person: bright blue eyes and jet-black hair, a scruffy two-day-old beard that I found—oddly enough—attractive. *I usually go for the pretty ones.*

Why do I even care? I don't know the guy, I thought, goofily. *And while I'm focused on my recovery, the last thing I need to do is develop the hots for Sammy's big brother.*

"Oh yeah. This is my girlfriend, Opal. Opal, meet my sister, Sammy." Rob grinned.

Opal stuck out a perfectly manicured hand toward Sammy. She was wearing an unusual owl ring that was so large, it covered three fingers. Sammy stared at her hand for several seconds and I had to look away. *Cringy.*

Finally, Sammy accepted Opal's handshake. "Well, he's never mentioned you to me," she said.

Ouch.

Opal's eyes narrowed for a second, a flash of something like pure disdain on her face, before it morphed back into a placid smile.

"Well, I've heard a lot about you, Sammy. And I hope we can be dear friends," she said, with a sickly-sweet smile.

"Definitely," Sammy replied, through clenched teeth. Then she looked over at me as though for help. I shrugged. *Who cares if Rob brought his girlfriend? That's his business, not ours.*

Remembering the journal wedged in the back of my pants, all I wanted to do in that moment, though, was break away from the current drama and read more of it in private in my own room.

Sounds from the kitchen had halted moments ago, and I imagined Mia on the other side of the wall, listening carefully to each word.

It was no secret: *for a while, she had been obsessed with Rob. Until he'd broke her heart.*

But he's obviously moved on and so should she, I thought, tiredly, looking at sweet little Opal on the couch.

Opal gave Rob a weary side-eye, as though waiting for

him to say something more. She sighed. "We work together at Spinelli's. That's how we met. We've been dating for, like, six months. Right, honey?"

Rob rubbed his beard. "Yeah, I think that's right."

Silence dragged on for several seconds, until I felt compelled to end it.

"Have you two picked out a room already?" I asked Rob, shifting in my seat. The journal was sliding around my backside, poking me painfully in the kidney.

Opal spoke for him again: "We put our stuff in the first room, but we can move it if you all would prefer. There's a big bedroom on this floor. I figured Sammy might want it. It has a bath attached. An amazing claw-foot tub…" She gave Sammy a hopeful smile.

Sammy stood up, stretching. She was obviously annoyed, and normally I'd be more interested in the unfolding drama, but all I wanted to do was retreat to my room and read the strange, secret journal I'd found. *What was that name again … Elena? It sounded so familiar…*

"You know what? You guys are the only couple here, so why don't you take the master bedroom? The girls and I will stay in the four rooms upstairs. It's only fitting considering we'll be busy hanging out and doing artwork stuff. Plus, you two deserve your privacy," Sammy said.

There was a loud, metallic bang in the kitchen, followed by a few more.

I looked over at Riley and raised my eyebrows, teasingly. She'd been quiet since running into Rob and Opal upstairs. She'd screamed loud enough to give me a heart attack earlier, but she seemed calm as a clam now.

Riley smiled tightly back at me.

Rob said, "Are you sure, Sammy? We don't mind staying upstairs…"

"I'd prefer you two downstairs on your own," Sammy replied, stiffly.

"Well, it's settled then. I can't wait to soak in that big ol' tub, right, honey?" Opal nudged Rob.

Another bang in the kitchen.

This is going to be a long three months, I realized.

Chapter Sixteen

Sammy

I chose the bedroom at the end of the hallway upstairs, as far from my brother and Opal as possible. *Why does he always have to be so selfish?* I thought, bitterly, dumping clothes and toiletries out of my bag on the bed.

The bed was dusty, but neatly made. I hadn't pulled back the heavy duvet yet, afraid of what might lie beneath the cover and sheets. But the room itself had an old, magnificent fireplace to my left and a tall blond armoire with ornate flowers and stars carved in the wood on my right. There was a window facing the sea and, from here, I could see the sun finally shifting over the water, making it blue and lustrous, the sea calm and smooth as glass despite the earlier signs of a storm.

At least Opal will keep Rob entertained, so I don't have to. The important thing is that my brother is here with me, and he's safe. No one can reach us here…

I threw open the doors of the armoire, nose tickling from the smell of mold and dust. *Not going to put my clothes in there until after I clean it.*

Instead, I stacked my clothes in the corner of the room on the floor, organizing them in socks, shirts, and shorts. I made a tiny pile of panties. *That's the best I can do for now.*

Riley had chosen the room next to mine and Scarlett had chosen the one across the hall. That left Mia with the first room, the one Rob and Opal had been occupying for the last couple days.

Yikes.

Mia was still downstairs in the kitchen, totally ignoring us all, preparing her famous chili. Although Mia and I had grown up in quite different households, we were both well versed in caring for ourselves. Her dad was usually out of the picture, her mom always focused on her latest artwork. And Rob and I … well, we'd learned to fend for ourselves.

I knew my friends thought our relationship was odd. Technically, Rob was three years my senior. But I'd been the only one capable of good decisions back then, and I'd been less of a sister and more of a parent to him, for as long as I could remember. As a teen, he was sneaky: selling dope behind my back, hiding truancy letters from school.

Now I'm the one hiding something. But at least I'm safe here on the island. No one knows I'm here, and I won't have to worry about them hurting Rob to get to me…

I tried to imagine what my friends would think if they knew the truth: my real reason for coming to the island. *They probably never would have agreed to come in the first place...*

I removed my laptop from my backpack and a few of my sketches. As eager as I was to get to work on some of my designs, I couldn't shake this overwhelming cloud of exhaustion. Whether it was from the long journey to get here, or the weight of carrying my secrets alone, I couldn't be sure.

I'll just rest for a moment.

Curling into a ball on top of the covers, I let the grumble of thunder in the distance soothe me to sleep. Somewhere in the back of my mind, I could hear the words *if you don't come up with the money within forty-eight hours, you will pay.*

You will pay. Those three words ricocheted in my brain like bullets. *Pay, how?* I wondered.

As of forty-eight hours ago, that deadline had passed. *Surely, the consequences of my actions couldn't reach me here...*

Chapter Seventeen

Riley

With Sammy and Scarlett in their rooms—unpacking, I presumed—and Rob and his girlfriend moved over to the master downstairs, I crept down the spiral staircase and made my way to the kitchen.

Rising from the butcher-block kitchen table, Mia sighed theatrically. "Are you hungry? The chili's almost done. I like to let it simmer, but I could pour you a bowl if you're ready..."

I shook my head. "I'll wait till it's done simmering. No worries."

The kitchen, unlike the rest of the house, looked fairly new and modern. Like an oddly made patchwork quilt, the house was a mixture of old and new. The cabinets were an old-timey lime-green color, but clean and spotless. The double ovens and kitchen island looked as though they'd never been used, and they were expensive.

Following my gaze, Mia said, "I thought we would need more stuff. Utensils and pans, silverware and dishes... I figured it would take us a week of traveling on- and offshore to get this place prepared. But it's almost like they left it all behind... Look."

She walked over to one of the drawers and opened it, then started opening and closing cabinets. She was right; the shelves were lined with expensive-looking china. The drawers were lined neatly with utensils and measuring cups of every size.

"Whoever lived here liked to cook."

"You can say that again," Mia sighed, snapping one of the cabinets shut. She turned and leaned against the counter, crossing her arms over her chest.

"So, what's she look like?"

"Who?" But I already knew who she meant. *The perfect Mia Ludlow jealous of another girl?* Internally, I cringed. "Didn't you see her yourself?"

Mia shook her head. "I was so surprised to see him that I rushed off without really noticing. It was such a blur. I mean, I knew he would be here, but I thought I'd have a full day to prepare, and I never expected him to bring a girl. Although I probably should have..." Her voice dropped several decibels as though she was just now realizing that the couple were down the hall, within earshot.

"She's pretty, I guess. In that tries-too-hard sort of way,"

I said, my voice barely above a whisper. As I said it, I felt self-conscious about my own clothes and makeup. *It takes one try-hard to know another, I guess.* For me, I didn't really have a choice in the matter. My face and hair were so plain that I needed all the help I could get. Opal, on the other hand, looked overdone. She was gorgeous and didn't need any help, although I'd never admit that to Mia.

Truth was, I didn't have time to worry about beauty and fame like my friends; I didn't have the same luxury, barely affording my final semester at Monroe. For me, it was school and puzzles and … memories. I didn't have time to think about a boyfriend, or worry how pretty I looked…

Mia nodded, as though that settled it. She picked up a white soup spoon and stirred the heavy pot full of chili.

"It smells wonderful." I bent over the pot, peering inside. "I don't think I've ever had chili without meat before, but I'm excited to try it."

It smelled delicious, even if it was made with tinned tomatoes, beans, and sauce.

"We'll head into town tomorrow. Pick up some meat and other supplies. Maybe we could go together? We'll learn to steer that dinky little boat," Mia said, with a grin.

"Sounds like a plan."

Thunder rolled, giving the foundation of the house a sturdy shake. Mia shivered, but I loved storms—*a good downpour will help me sleep tonight, help drown out the demons inside me.*

"We should leave this here and go explore, while

everyone else is busy. Before the rain comes," Mia suggested.

"Okay."

While Mia went upstairs to change, I stirred the chili for her then wandered around the first floor, getting a good look at the place.

Off the kitchen, there were two rooms—the living room and a narrow dining space. I walked past the pictures on the mantel, barely glancing at the faces.

Down a narrow corridor were three doors. The door to the master suite was closed; through the thick wooden door, I could hear Rob and Opal talking in hushed voices.

I got as close to their door as I dared, but still couldn't make out what they were saying. It almost sounded like they were ... arguing about something, whisper-shouting through the walls...

The other doors led to a small half bath and a large washroom. There was an ancient washer and dryer, covered in dust. I don't know what possessed me to do so, but I popped open the lid on the washer.

There were clothes inside; I scrunched up my nose, the smell of moldy, forgotten garments invading my nostrils.

"Ready?"

I jumped back, pulling the lid shut.

Mia had changed into a black and brown jumpsuit with palm trees printed all over it. *It seems very fitting for an island getaway trip, unlike her usual messy paint clothes.*

"Yep." As we exited the washroom, we both looked toward the closed bedroom door. I put a finger in my mouth, mimicking gagging. It was childish of me, but Mia threw her head back and gave me that famous belly laugh of hers.

We ran outside, giggling so hard our bellies ached. Thunder rolled; bulgy-black clouds spread like bruises in the sky.

"Fuck Rob!" Mia gasped as soon as we were far enough from the house. "Worthless ass."

"You're way too good for him," I told her.

"You know what? You're right. I'm going to pretend he's not here, him and what's-her-face, and focus on my painting. I'll create my best work yet while I'm here."

Pellets of rain came tumbling down as we made our way toward the boat dock.

The water looked angry, lapping up the sides of the island. Being here, away from my stuffy apartment and distracting studies, felt right somehow...

"I know next to nothing about Alaska, but I wonder what sort of sea life is out there?" Mia said.

"Hmmm. Probably some beluga whales. Maybe dolphins and sharks," I said.

Mia looked out at the water, shielding her eyes, even though there was no sun shining anymore.

"It's strange, isn't it?"

"What?"

"Being so far away from civilization. Everywhere you

look, there's water. Almost like we're the last people left on earth," Mia said, softly.

"Well," I said, "if it's the last place on earth, then I'm glad to be here with you."

Mia turned to me and in a moment that caught me off guard, she reached over and threw her arms around me. I put my hands around her shoulders, rubbing gentle circles on her back.

"I'm so glad we met, Riley. Truly I am."

"Me too," I said, and I meant it with all my heart.

Chapter Eighteen

Mia

"This place is strange. Who do you think lived out here?" Riley asked.

We had escaped the sluices of rainfall by slipping inside the cottage, located behind the house.

"No clue," I said, running my hands over the motheaten mattress and stack of books.

"Oh, I know that one," Riley said, pointing at a book in the stack. "It's an old mystery about a group of people who go to an island and start getting killed off one by one."

I rolled my eyes. "You can't be serious, Rye."

Riley laughed. "No, seriously. It's a classic. You've never read Agatha Christie?"

I picked up the book, turning it over and back in my hands. "I guess whoever stayed here had a sense of humor, huh? I don't think I'd want to read something like that while I'm stranded out here on an island."

Riley shrugged. "We're not exactly stranded. We have a boat."

I shrugged. Boat or not, I saw no reason to leave, other than to get more supplies. With rumors recirculating about my past and the anniversary date, I had no interest in returning home for a good long while. *Maybe I'll never go back...*

I walked over to the one window in the cottage; I tried to look out, but the windows were sooty and dark, too hard to see. "Think it's slowed down out there yet? I want to go look at the building in the back we haven't seen yet."

"Should be. It sounds more like a trickle and less of a pour out there now," Riley murmured.

"Maybe we should give it a few more minutes." I picked up another book from the stack. It, too, looked like some sort of murder mystery.

"I know you hate Rob and all, but maybe he can tell us more about his friend, the guy whose relatives owned this place..." Riley said.

"Yeah. I guess."

"It seems like a strange place, one with some history to it," Riley commented.

"You think? I don't know why it never occurred to me to look up info online about Whisper Island; I guess I've been too focused on getting here, and my current projects." I didn't say what I really wanted: that sticking around town wasn't good for me. Like Sammy, I had my own things to hide…

The rain had stopped, temporarily, so we slipped out of the stuffy cottage. Farther down the footpath, the woods grew thicker and darker.

"You think there's any animals that live on this island?" Riley said behind me, her words so close to the back of my neck that I shuddered as she said them.

I stopped walking, looking around the trees and shrubbery for animals. *Is she trying to freak me out?* I thought, feeling slightly annoyed.

We kept going. Nearly half a mile from the cottage, we found the final building on the far side of the island. It was long and eerie, at the crest of a steep hill, windows sooty and dark.

"This definitely looks nothing like the pictures we saw online," I said.

"I know, right?" Riley said.

As we approached the wide door on one end of the building, we immediately noticed the thick padlock. *What the hell?*

"We'll need a sledgehammer to get that off. Unless there's another way in," Riley said.

The gray paint was peeling, the roof caving in on top.

I rattled the lock back and forth, growling with frustration.

"I don't see any other way in. Although, if I had to guess, this building's going to be useless to us. It's probably empty, like that other storage building," Riley said.

"Probably." Although I couldn't help feeling a little disappointed. *There's something about locked spaces that gives me the creeps.*

A flash of lightning struck the sky, illuminating the main house in the distance like a ghoulish shadow in the dark. The waves of the sea were choppy and black; I tried not to think about how isolated we were out here.

"Storm's definitely coming. Let's get back."

It wasn't nearly nighttime, yet the sun was hidden behind the clouds, the sky so dark that it was difficult to find the footpath.

"Wait for me," Riley said, moving her stubby legs to catch up with mine. Side by side, we navigated down the path leading to the house.

We were nearly at the abandoned cottage when another strike of lightning hit nearby.

"Oh my God. Mia, stop. You have to stop."

I froze in my tracks, the panic in Riley's voice making my stomach do a backflip. One at a time, the hairs on the back of my neck stood on end.

"I-I saw something. At least I think I did."

My throat tightened. "Like, an animal?" I had no idea what sort of wildlife could exist on an island like this. Instantly, my brain leapt to the worst possibility—*aren't there polar bears in Alaska?*

Riley took a step off the path, stopping and staring into the dark thicket of brush and trees.

"What is it?" I asked, exasperated.

"Not an animal. I thought I saw … bones."

"Excuse me. Did you say bones?"

Right on cue, another bolt of lightning struck the sky. I tried to catch a glimpse of what she might be seeing, but I couldn't see a thing anymore.

"There. Right there!" Riley was walking now, shimmying around two trees. I took a few steps forward, stopping to take out my cell phone. I turned on my flashlight app, and with a shaky hand, I held it up in front of my face.

"See? What the hell is that?" Riley squatted on her haunches by something on the ground.

Tentatively, I walked towards her, trying to see it too. When Riley stood back up and stepped to the side, I finally understood. On the ground by her feet rested a human skull.

Chapter Nineteen

Scarlett

I followed the sing-song cries of laughter, stepping quietly down the spiral staircase to join my friends. I'd been in my room for over an hour—not napping but reading the journal.

I was still haunted by the words it contained:

Elena Blackwater was the first to die. Many more will follow.

Who was the writer of the journal? A fantasist, creating stories for her own amusement? And why am I assuming the writer was a woman? It very well could have been a man.

Most importantly: *who is Elena Blackwater? And why does that name ring a bell?*

My brain was scrolling through images etched there— blogs, social media pages, current news… *Why why why do I know that name?*

The only person who I knew might have some answers for me was Rob. After all, it was his friend's family who owned Whisper Island.

I found him in the kitchen, sitting at the butcher-block table beside Opal, shoveling a heaped spoonful of Mia's vegetarian chili into his mouth. Sammy leaned against the counter, smiling. It was her laugh that I'd heard earlier— that contagious, deep-throated chuckle I knew too well. She looked better than she had before, rested, her cheeks doughy and pink with pleasure, as though being around her brother brought out the best in her.

"What did I miss?" I said, walking over to the pot of chili on the stove. I leaned over and took a whiff. Mia was the only person I knew who could make mean vegetarian soups. It was one thing she and I had in common—our loathing for meat.

"You didn't miss anything. I was just telling Rob and Opal that story about Mr. Grossman. Remember when he fell asleep in class and had that dream, the one about finding treasure?"

I nodded. "How could I forget? He kept muttering, 'They're rare. How much could this booty be worth?'"

Sammy was laughing again. So were Rob and Opal. "I know I'm funny, but I'm not that funny. What the hell have you guys been drinking without me, huh?"

"Oh, not much. Just a little of this." Opal held up a flask. "Cinnamon whiskey. Want a sip?"

I walked over and took a deep swallow, then handed it back to her. "Thanks, Opal." *Drinking probably wasn't a good idea, but it might help with kicking the pills … one step at a time…*

I walked back over to the stove and filled a deep white bowl with Mia's chili. Somehow, it felt traitorous to drink and laugh with Rob and Opal, knowing how badly he'd broken Mia's heart. *Speaking of Mia, where is she? And Riley…*

"Where's everyone else?" I asked, casually, carrying my bowl over to the table to join Rob and Opal. Since arriving, I hadn't had much appetite. *But forcing down some food might help.*

Sammy was cleaning now, wiping down counters with a thick brown dishrag.

Rob and Opal shrugged, digging into Mia's chili.

"I think they went out to look around at the other buildings. Knowing Mia, she's already putting together a game plan for tomorrow. I know she wants to clean up this place and take the boat to town for more food," Sammy rambled. Her words were slurred. She always was a lightweight when it came to drinking.

I stood up and went to the back-bay windows, looking out at the dark trees and stormy weather outside. I thought about the cottage where I found the book. *Could there be other journals out there? Why didn't I look around better while I was out there? Elena Blackwater … I know that name…*

"If they're not back soon, we should go look for them. It's looking nasty out there," I said, absentmindedly.

Sammy waved me off with her rag in hand. "They're fine, Scarlett. Probably poking around, exploring." She caught my eye. "Mia probably wanted some time to do her own thing," she said in a hushed voice, giving a knowing nod in Rob and Opal's direction.

Internally, I was rolling my eyes. *If Sammy really cared about Mia's feelings for Rob, she never would have invited him here in the first place.*

Speaking of Rob…

"Hey, can you tell me a little more about this place? I'd love to know Whisper Island's back story, Rob." I resumed my seat at the table, stirring my chili and blowing steam from the top of it. What I really wanted was a line or a pill, not an innocuous bowl of chili…

Rob looked up, seemingly startled by my question. "Honestly, I don't know much at all." He stared at me, curious, as though he were seeing me for the first time.

Slowly, his eyes drifted down from my lips and centered on my chest.

"Well, I'd love to know what little you do know," I said, leaning forward with my cleavage and moving my lips slow. I had to admit, Rob was sexy as hell, and looked nothing at all like Sammy with her dull, prudish style. His lips were fuller, his eyes bigger, and more alive. And he had these dimples on his cheeks, almost joker-esque and naughty when he smiled.

Opal was watching us, eyes flitting back and forth. Almost like she could sense Rob's attraction to me. I pretended she wasn't there.

That's the thing about being a pretty girl; I'm used to getting attention. And when a man wants me, I can always pick up on it right away. My own little special gift.

Rob pushed his bowl to the side with a clank and sat up straighter. "My buddy Manny is the one whose family owned this place."

"What is Manny's last name?" I pressed. *Elena Blackwater was the first to die.*

"Rodriguez. But I'm not sure which members of his family lived here though. Distant relatives, maybe...?"

"What happened to the family? Do you know?"

Rob shook his head. "No idea. All I know is that his parents were given the property and he said we could use it for the summer. No tragic back stories that I know of, if that's what you're thinking..."

Sammy was about to say something else when the front door opened with a bang. I heard a rush of voices, excited and upset.

When Mia and Riley entered the kitchen, they were drenched from head to toe and wide-eyed.

"What? What's happened?" I asked, pushing my seat back and rising to my feet.

"We found something beside that old cottage out there. It looks like a human skull," Mia said, wildly.

Chapter Twenty

Riley

O ne by one, my fellow islanders trotted through the fog and rain, Mia at the helm.

As we scurried along, Opal shouted through the rain, trying to come up with any excuse she could to explain away the skull.

"You can buy human skulls online. Furthermore, you can buy props that look just like skulls," she claimed.

"And why the hell would someone do that?" Mia snapped, stopping on the path and causing Scarlett to run right into her.

Opal shrank back from the question, embarrassed, but when Mia turned around and started moving again, I saw Opal's face curl up in disgust. *She obviously knows Mia is Rob's ex,* I realized.

"It's right over here," Mia said. She made a sharp turn, veering off the path, tracing the same steps we'd taken earlier.

One at a time, we formed a circle around it. I held up my flashlight app again, letting the whole group see the eerie gray skull in the dark.

"Jesus." Sammy covered her mouth in horror.

Rob bent down beside the skull, and Opal followed suit. "Shine it closer so we can get a good look," Rob said.

I knelt down beside him, pressing the light as close to the skeletal face as I dared.

"That sure as shit looks real to me," Opal said, breathless.

"Who does it belong to?" Scarlett gasped. But when I looked up at her, she wasn't looking at the skull; rather, she was staring westward, over at the dilapidated cottage Mia and I had inspected earlier.

"No idea. There's no other bones around," I said, evenly.

"Just the head." Scarlett wrapped her arms around herself, gasping for air.

"Hey, it's okay. Breathe… It's just a skull. It can't hurt us." I reached for her, but she lurched back, eyes still darting between the skull and the cottage.

Why is she acting so paranoid? I wondered.

Opal stood, dusting off her skinny jeans. In the heady glow of my flashlight app, she looked younger than I had realized, and ghoulishly pale.

"Like I said," Opal said, "this could be a skull that

someone placed here. I mean, think about it, guys—someone who lives on an island loves the sea, right? What would be cooler than using skulls or pirate motifs or treasure as decorations?"

My mind flickered back to earlier, that skull tattoo on her foot. "Does that look like a fake skull to you?"

Opal stared at the skull, then slowly shook her head back and forth.

"I'm not afraid of whose skull it is, I'm afraid of who put it there." Scarlett's voice was so tiny in the dark, I barely caught her words.

Mia walked over; unlike me, Scarlett let her in, and she whispered quiet, soothing words in the dark. I looked away, a twinge of resentment brewing deep inside me.

"It could have washed up from the sea, or it could have been out here for a long time. Maybe a vagrant who was staying on the island and died here," Rob suggested.

"Real or fake, we have to contact the police immediately," Sammy said.

Mia's eyes widened in the dark. "Really? And how do you expect to do that out here? We don't have cell service and it's too dark to take the boat out tonight. The shore is ten miles from here, and they'll call it a crime scene and whisk us back to shore, probably permanently."

"We should wait until morning," I said, sternly. "I'd like to get a better look at this thing then, anyhow. Then we can make our decision." The last thing I wanted was to leave the island, but I could understand the others' fears.

"Well, if we want to get a better look, why don't we carry it inside?" Opal suggested.

We all turned our heads toward her with a look of disgust.

"We can't touch it. The police might want to investigate it, search for clues…" I said.

"Then let's head in for the night and lock the doors. We need to go into town in the morning for supplies anyway. We'll find out who we need to talk with from the local police department when we take the boat out tomorrow," Mia sighed.

It was not only our best plan; it was the only one we had at the time.

Chapter Twenty-One

Mia

There was a faint crack in the ceiling above my bed.

I imagined the skull out there on the island, hidden among the trees. *Bones snapping apart, splitting crevices. Blood and vomit soaking through carpet, eyes pleading for help...*

Shuddering, I pushed the covers aside and groaned as I sat up in bed. The sheets stank of rot and mildew. But it wasn't the smell or the eerie groans in the walls that kept me up past 1am. It was that skull—and, selfishly, what the discovery of the skull might mean for my own plans. Because, despite what the girls and everyone else at school thought about me, I was never going to be my mother. Cristal Ludlow was a natural talent; I had to work for mine, every single day, and it had been that way since I was in diapers. Always one step behind my mother. Always trying to find a way to walk in her shoes. Mainly, I wanted to impress her.

She laughed when I told her I had applied to Monroe. My father wasn't supportive either.

True artists make art, Mimi Girl. They don't need to go to some fancy college and earn a degree. No one can give you permission to do art but you. That degree is your permission slip; rip it up, Mimi. Tear down those silly ideas you have about what it takes to reach true mastery.

That was easy for her to say. My mother grew up in a wealthy family and even though she liked to brag about not attending college and being "self-taught," I had it on good authority (from my father) that my grandparents' house was full of servants, including full-time art and music teachers. She had a gift, undoubtedly, but privilege early in life helped her cultivate it. *I guess people could say the same thing about me.*

Even when I finally earned a full-ride scholarship for university, my mother barely reacted.

Go if you must, she said, as though I had disappointed her.

As though I were leaving home to join a cult instead of attending a prestigious art college. *Go if you must, Mimi.*

And now that my college career was over, she was quick to point out: *you should be selling paintings, darling. I did my first show at twenty-two, much younger than you are now.*

But my mother didn't have to overcome the same bad

reputation I'd earned my first year at Monroe; and she didn't know what it felt like trying to re-earn respect and forge my own path outside her spotlight.

When I told my mother about Whisper Island, she was excited. For the first time in a long time, I saw a flicker of approval behind her eyes.

Of course, I knew she would be. This bohemian idea of artists giving up everything and running off to strange places for the sake of art was something my mother could get behind.

But when I told her about the others, that expression of admiration slowly melted away.

Art is individual, Mimi. It's not a collaborative experience. What do you even know about these young women? What sort of talents do they have?

I hated her in that moment. Because those "women" were more of a family to me than she had ever been. And I loved the idea of coming out here to enjoy what might be our last summer together before starting our "real" lives.

I backtracked, trying to explain it to her, when what I really should have done was get up and leave. My mother never had anything to offer except criticism and heartache.

But I tried, as I always do, to prove my worth to my mother.

Oh, mom. You should meet them. Especially Riley. She is a freaking genius. The intricacy with which she works, the painstaking details when she's cutting, forming die casts to create the perfect pieces...

But my mother broke in with laughter, reminding me that puzzle-making was a dying art.

She's not wrong. Not completely.

Nowadays, most puzzles are manufactured. Only a handful of people in the world do them by hand.

Which was another reason I liked Riley. Something about her reminded me of my mother, the parts of my mother I loved—the tenacity, the sheer focus, the attention to detail, the not giving a damn what others were working on or what was trending... All she cared about was making puzzles.

I flipped on my bedside lamp. Dull yellow light cast shadows on the ceiling and walls.

I listened for sounds from the others—*how did they fall asleep so easily after what we found?*

Moving to the window that overlooked the back of the house, I parted the curtains and looked out in the night. The skull was barely a few hundred feet from here, but all I could see in the window was my own ghoulish reflection staring back at me through the glass.

I wondered who the skull belonged to. But more, I wondered what this meant for our little vacation.

Tomorrow we would take the boat out and return to the mainland. We were supposed to be picking up some food and cleaning supplies—but now our only plan was to find the local police department and report what we had found.

If the island becomes a crime scene, then we'll surely have to leave. *And I can't go back home again. I can't face any more reminders of what I've done…*

It could take days, weeks, or even months for them to allow us to come back to the island…

If a crime occurred here, then we will be forced to catch a plane back home. And then I'll have to face the anniversary of my biggest mistake and read those headlines again, just like I did five years ago…

I shut the curtains and felt around on the floor beside the bed for my shoes. There was no way I could sleep after what happened. I needed to do something … something specific.

I needed to paint. Needed to shut the part of my brain off that was so often filled with worry and dread and open the part that allowed my brush to soar across the canvas, creating its own version of reality.

At home, in mine and Sammy's apartment, I had my own special space in my room where I set up my canvas and laid out my paints and brushes and cloths. I was ritualistic with my methods. But here … I didn't have that. I'd brought some canvasses and paint, but I'd put them out in the first storage building when we arrived, planning to work out there when I could get away from the others.

Kicking myself for leaving them outside, I made a quick decision—*I'll go fetch them.*

A little fresh air might do me some good. And whatever, or whoever, that skull belonged to … that must have happened long ago, before we arrived…

We are alone on the island. I have nothing to worry about, I assured myself.

I opened the door of my bedroom a crack and stuck my head out. I glanced up and down the dark hallway. All was quiet now, the other girls' doors firmly shut, no light flooding from underneath.

I dragged my hands along the wall, feeling my way through the dark. At last, I came to the edge of the top step.

Not wanting to wake the others and feeling oddly criminal for sneaking outside by myself this late, I stepped down slowly on the first step. The wood creaked heavily beneath my foot, and I cringed.

Fuck it. Who cares if I wake them up? We'll probably all be leaving for good tomorrow and I want—NEED—to create something before I go.

The living room was dark, but soft light flooded in from the kitchen. The faces in the photos on the mantle grinned eerily at me in the dark.

I stopped, making sure no one else was up, and peered down the hallway on the first floor that led to the master bedroom.

Startled to find the door open, I stepped back into the shadowy living room. A soft peal of laughter drifted from the room. My jaw tensed, as I thought about Rob with his new girl. *What was her stupid name? Oh yeah, Opal.*

Opal was lovely, as much as it pained me to admit it. Tonight, standing out there in the dark by the skull, I had a chance to get a real good look at her. With her ballerina body and posture, she almost reminded me of... I shuddered, forcing away memories that bulged inside me.

I heard the laughter again; it sounded like a little girl, snorting and giggling with Rob in the dark. My eyes grew watery as I marched right out the front door.

Chapter Twenty-Two

Scarlett

W hen I opened my eyes and looked at my phone on the pillow beside me, I was shocked to see it was three o'clock in the morning. Usually, I was a deep sleeper; it took a lot to get a rise from me before 8am. *Something must have woken me; but what?*

Within seconds, the *what* came flooding back... *Oh God ... the journal, the skull... Nothing to take the edge off...*

Quickly, I sat up, holding a hand to my chest, gasping. I could feel that old urge returning. The tightening. The shallow breathing. The need for something to calm me. I remembered Riley's prescription for Xanax and in a moment of madness, I considered sneaking into her room and swiping a few.

No no no. I can't do that. I came here to cut myself off from the drugs ... to force myself to get, and stay, clean.

A chill ran up my spine as I remembered our earlier discovery.

Whose skull was it that we found tonight? Could there be someone out there lurking, someone living on the island ... the same someone who killed the owner of that wretched skull?

Elena Blackwater, the first one who died...

The journal was tucked between my mattress and box spring. I lifted myself out of bed, throwing my feet over the side, and stood up to retrieve it.

For a moment, I felt nothing ... but then the tips of my fingers grazed the soft leather. I wrested it out and turned on the overhead light in my room to read the next entry.

One by one, members of the group will disappear. There will be many, and then there will be none.

I shuddered at the realization that there were six of us on the island tonight. Did that count as *many*? Me, Riley, Mia, Sammy, Rob, and that girlfriend of his.

There were no dates listed on the vague journal entries. *Is it nonsense, written by a madman? Someone who was bored on the island, scribbling random thoughts down...? What if the writer of the journal is lying out there, their skull tucked in the sand and brush...?*

Unable to return to sleep, I put the journal back under my mattress and tightened my robe. The house was eerily quiet, not even the soft sounds of snoring or groaning from my bedmates next door.

I slipped out of my room and padded down the twisted stairwell, careful not to lose my footing in the dark.

As I reached the bottom, I was struck by the smell of smoke. Not the kind of smoke you get from a campfire or cigarettes, but something more familiar to me.

Instantly, I saw that the front door was ajar. Against my better judgment, I pushed it all the way open. A rush of icy cold air smacked me in the face, sucking the breath from my chest.

"Hey." I jumped at the sound of a man's voice coming from the front of the house.

The source of the smoke and the voice became clear. Rob was standing a few feet from the front porch in jeans and T-shirt, shivering as he lifted a pipe to his lips.

"What are you doing?" I whisper-shouted, quickly closing the front door behind me and stepping off the porch to join him.

Rob chuckled, struggling to hold the smoke in his lungs. "You're not going to tell on me, are you?"

My heart pounded in my chest as I stared at the pipe. "I can't believe you snuck drugs onto the plane. What the hell were you thinking?"

Rob laughed again. He offered the pipe to me. "I didn't bring it with me. I might be dumb, but I'm not that fucking dumb. I bought it off a guy inland before we got on the boat. Believe it or not, people like to get high everywhere, including Alaska."

I shook my head at the pipe, turning back toward the sea. *I can't believe it. I came all the way out here, traveling thousands of miles ... and here it is, right in my face. I'll never escape it. The only thing I can change is my choices, not the opportunities...*

I stared at the water, eyes blurring. I'd expected it to be rough at this time, but it looked smooth and clear, the moon casting a heady glow over the surface. Almost as though you could step off the edge and walk across it like a thick sheet of glass.

"Who am I kidding? Of course, you're going to tell. I'm the bad guy, right? Let me guess. Sammy said I was a fuck-up for a brother, and Mia told you I broke her heart. Am I right?"

I shrugged, turning back to him. My eyes floated back to the pipe, following it as it moved away from his mouth.

"I don't know. You tell me. Are they right about you?"

It was dark, but I could see him smiling, teeth glimmering white in the pale moonlight. I shuddered as I remembered the toothy rotting bones of the skull... *What if we're not safe out here? What do we really know about this place...?*

"Yeah, they're right. I have some issues with using, okay? Been on the wagon more times than I can count. Fallen off every fucking time. Shit happens."

"And Mia?" I asked, looking for shadows in the trees.

"Mia. Well, she's a great girl. She deserves a better man than me, that's for damn sure. I didn't mean to hurt her. We just weren't meant to be. Have you ever felt that way about someone? No matter how great they seem, you can't force yourself to feel something you don't…? You can't change no matter how you want to?"

"Yes, I do understand that." I reached for the pipe and lighter in his hand.

I could feel his eyes on me, watching carefully, as I lifted the pipe to my lips. I flicked the lighter at the bowl on the end, sucking in deeply as I matched his gaze.

Day Two

Chapter Twenty-Three

Sammy

In the darkness, it was impossible to see anything. Shadows emerged from the trees on the island, lengthening in size. Surpassing the tops of the trees. Hideous monsters, tall as mountains, skinny gray arms so long their knuckles dragged the forest floor. They moved toward me, spindly dark fingers reaching ... *closer closer closer.*

I arose with a theatrical scream. Gasping, I looked around at the wood-paneled walls, the hideous wardrobe in the corner... *It's okay. I'm safe here. It was just a dream.*

But then memories came flooding back...

The skull we found. The threats I received before leaving town...

What if the skull has something to do with me? What if

danger followed me to the island?... What if I've endangered my brother and my friends?

I shook my head. *There's no way anyone can find me here, right?*

The curtains were drawn. Surprised to discover it was already morning, I gathered up a change of clothes and slipped down the hall to the upstairs bathroom, trying to steady my breathing. *It was just a dream. And the skull can't be related to me, can it? It's so ... old-looking.*

As I stripped out of last night's grimy clothes, memories of the dream faded. By the time the pipes groaned to life, rusty lukewarm water spilling over my head and shoulders, I'd forgotten about the hideous monsters and pushed the fearful thoughts of danger as far away as I dared.

No matter how high I turned the water up, I couldn't get it warm, and the pressure was off—water pellets striking my skin one minute, then slowing to a trickle the next. I scrubbed quickly, then, shivering, I stepped out and wrapped a ratty old towel around me.

As I dressed, I could hear the others rustling around downstairs. The clatter of dishes, the soft murmur of voices. *For a moment, this felt like a normal trip with friends instead of a secret getaway...*

Knowing Mia, she was probably making eggs and imitation bacon. Although I couldn't smell anything cooking.

I had hoped to spend our first day shopping, cleaning,

and getting prepped to begin our work. But that was all thrown for a loop when we found the skull.

I cannot have contact with the police today. What if someone recognizes me? What if there's a warrant...?

Twisting my damp hair into a knot at the base of my skull, I carefully navigated the twisty steps and went to the kitchen to join the others.

I was surprised to find Riley, and only Riley, sitting at the butcher-block table. The table was covered in large sheets of trace paper. Riley's head was down, as she sketched furiously on the page. It was a puzzle design, a rather complex one, at least one thousand interlocking pieces.

When she finally noticed me, she looked up and smiled timidly.

"Been working on this all night," she said.

"It's incredible." I pulled out the chair beside her. "But where are the others?"

Riley's smile faded. "Opal's still in bed. Your brother mentioned that she's not feeling quite well. And everyone else—well, they're outside dealing with the boat issue."

"Boat issue?"

Riley carefully erased a line, then blew rubber off the page.

"There's a hole in it."

A hole?

"What do you mean?" I asked, dumbly.

"Mia was out there checking for life jackets and such

when she discovered a hole in the bottom. Water is already coming in. There's no way we can take it out until it's repaired."

My stomached tightened like a fist. The thought of being stranded on an island with no way off... *Oh God. What if someone punctured the boat on purpose?*

"Why do you look so damn calm then?" I asked, snapping more than I had intended. "Sorry."

Riley set her pencil down and scooted her chair back. "This is the only thing that calms me. I couldn't sleep at all because of that freakish skull... Who do you think it belonged to?"

"I don't know," I said, sucking in a deep breath. I couldn't shake the knock of fear in my chest. *If we don't have a boat, how can we leave this place?*

The thought of returning home to danger was terrifying, but being stuck here, stranded, with an eerie skull—I didn't like that idea either.

"I was just going to head back out there to see if I could help," Riley said. "I came in because I felt like I was getting in their way. I didn't mean to get so distracted, but I needed to get this design on paper before I lost it."

"It's okay," I sighed. I was often snappish with Riley; whether it was jealousy of her new friendship with the group, or irritation at her annoyingly laidback attitude, I couldn't be sure.

Together, we walked outside. It was sunny and fairly

warm, nearly 60 degrees. *Nothing like you'd expect from Alaska.*

I could see Mia and Scarlett, scooping water out of the boat with big green buckets. And beside the boat itself, down in the water, was my brother.

When she saw me approaching, Mia shot me a horrified look. We were a lot alike, and we had known each other a long time, and I knew she was as fearful as me. I worried about many things before coming to the island, mostly about what would happen if I didn't come ... but I'd never envisioned being stuck on an island without a boat. *And stuck with a strange, nameless skull to boot.*

"What's Rob doing?" I said, joining the girls on the dock. Riley was still hanging back. I felt a flicker of irritation as I thought back to her, only moments earlier, sketching away at the table instead of coming outside to help our friends. *What's her deal? And why didn't anyone wake me up?* Although she seemed sweet enough, Riley also struck me as flighty and strange at times. *Scarlett likes her and so does Mia, so I guess that leaves me no choice but to do the same,* I thought, with a sigh.

"He's trying to patch the hole using some resin we had with our workshop supplies," Scarlett said. She looked positively ghoulish, purplish half-moons under her eyes. I got the sense that she didn't sleep much either.

"Let me help." I shot an annoyed look over at Riley as I snatched up one of the buckets.

"You shouldn't be in the water. It's way too cold. You'll catch pneumonia," I shouted at Rob.

"Okay, Mom." Rob dipped his head over the side of the boat and frowned at me.

"Don't give me that look. It's true," I said.

"Well, luckily, I brought a wetsuit with me. I'll be fine. But if we don't fix this hole, we won't be. I don't know about you guys, but I don't want to be stuck out here, rotting away like that corpse we found."

Scarlett let out a tiny gasp.

I wanted to correct my brother: *it wasn't a corpse; it was just an old skull.* But he was right: *if we couldn't find a way off the island and couldn't call out for help, how long would we be stuck out here?*

I felt my own fear rising to match Scarlett's. She looked bug-eyed and strange. "You okay?" I tried to ask her, but she brushed me off.

As the three of us tried to get the water out of the boat, Rob bobbled up and down beside it, trying to make the repair.

"I can't believe such a tiny hole could cause this big of a leak so fast," he said, gasping for air. His lips and cheeks looked blue. I had no idea what the water temperature was but based on the icy cold buckets we were dumping it was way too damn cold down there, like I said. *Wet suit or no wet suit, I don't want my brother getting sick or hurt out here.*

What if he gets sick and I can't get him off the island to see a doctor?

"I don't get it," Riley finally spoke, softly. She was still staring numbly at the boat, not helping, her hands tucked in her jacket pockets. Face twisted with confusion.

"Get what? And why aren't you helping?" Mia shouted, tossing water with a loud splash, barely missing Riley.

Riley, suddenly realizing how rude she was being, scooped up an empty bucket off the ground. But instead of helping, she held it in front of her, still gazing at the boat, looking back and forth from Rob to me.

"The hole is new. It must be," she said, absently. "Because ... well, there wasn't any water in the boat yesterday when we arrived. I checked it out when I came to the dock..."

"Could have happened last night while it was storming. Or maybe the boat's been rotting in that one spot, and it just finally broke free. Lucky us," Mia huffed, trying to be the voice of reason.

But Riley's words were sinking in... *What if someone pierced a hole in the boat on purpose? The same someone who left that skull for us to find... Could this have something to do with the mess I caused back home...?*

Riley shook her head, slowly, back and forth. "No way. What are the odds of that happening to this boat, on our very first night on the island?"

I stopped scooping; wiped sweat from my brow.

"Riley's right. It doesn't make sense," I admitted. *And it didn't. How the hell did this happen?*

The thought of someone else on the island with us,

watching through the trees, sabotaging our only ride off the island…

"Do you really think someone did this?" Mia asked, looking from one face to the next.

"I do. I think there's someone out here with us," Scarlett whimpered.

Chapter Twenty-Four

Riley

The more I thought about it, the more convinced I became.

Someone messed with our boat.

But who? And why?

That was the part I couldn't figure out. After an hour of working to fix the hole, we discovered nearly a dozen tiny holes scattered throughout. I couldn't tell how they'd been created. *By damage or by someone using some sort of sharp tool to create small punctures, perhaps?* I wondered. But, again, that led me back to: *who?*

Finally, we had removed enough water to hook up a rope and pull it onto shore. After it dried completely, we would have to examine it, marking all the holes. *I only hope it can be repaired. If not ... we could all be stuck for a while until a boat comes near and offers to help...*

But this was a secluded part of the ocean. Come to think of it, we hadn't seen one other boat since Juan and his helpers had left us.

"Doesn't look like we're going anywhere for a while. At least not today," I said, standing with my hands on my hips beside the overturned boat. It was barely noon, and I was already exhausted, especially considering that I'd barely slept all night, spending most of it working on my new puzzle. I was trying to remain as positive as possible, but this made it hard. It was too early for the girls to start freaking out, wanting to go home ... *but who could blame them if someone was sabotaging our boat?*

"Thanks for that news bulletin, Captain Obvious," Sammy said, turning back to the house. I watched the back of her head as she stomped off, realizing, not for the first time, that she didn't like me much. Truth was, I was starting to dislike her too.

Mia gave me an apologetic smile. "Ignore Sammy. She gets angry when she's anxious. We can fix this. Can't we?" Her voice shook as she asked it, unsure.

"I hope so," I said quietly.

Rob had gone inside earlier, to warm up and change back into normal clothes. As he crossed the island, dressed in a clean sweatshirt and jeans, Mia turned away and followed Sammy, not meeting his eye.

"Mia really hates me, doesn't she?" Rob had said,

flashing a gleaming smile at Scarlett and me. He was handsome and cunning; that Casanova style that some girls were drawn to, but not me.

"She doesn't hate you. She's worried about the boat. We all are," Scarlett said, cheeks finally gaining some color back as she looked at Rob. She batted her lashes, and he smiled sneakily back at her, as though there were some sort of secret between the two.

Oh, for fuck's sake, Scarlett.

Pretending I didn't notice their exchange, I excused myself and walked back to the house. It would take a while for the boat to dry, and if we patched it effectively, another day or two beyond that. The girls weren't going to like that, but there was nothing we could do at this point.

I considered the three men who had brought us. They had seemed friendly enough, and we'd paid them well— very well—to bring us. They would have no reason to return to the island and mess with our boat. *But if not them, then who?*

The thought of it being one of us concerned me… *Who else could have a motive for not wanting to leave the island?*

We truly were isolated out here on Whisper Island, which was our entire point of coming. *Would it be so bad if we had to wait a few days to return to the mainland for supplies? We still have plenty of stuff here.*

Inside, I could hear Mia and Sammy shuffling around the kitchen, opening and closing cabinets.

"Everything okay?"

Sammy's eyes were wide and frightened, but when I spoke, she narrowed them at me.

"Of course everything's not okay, Riley. There's a skeleton on the island, someone fucked with our boat, and we don't really have much food."

"Sammy, stop," Mia hushed, looking guiltily over at me.

"It's okay. She's right. I know this sucks, but I think I can get the boat repaired in a day or two. Surely, we have enough food for a few days, right? I mean, I know we brought plenty of canned vegetables and beans..."

Mia nodded, looking over at Sammy. "We have enough leftover chili for tonight. And plenty of canned food and ramen packs. That's why we brought along some rations with us, remember? We will be fine."

Sammy sighed heavily. She rested her backside against the counter, rubbing her face in her hands. "This just isn't the way I pictured it, you know. I didn't know Rob was bringing a girl, Mia. I swear it. And I certainly didn't plan for this..."

"Of course you didn't." Mia reached for her friend, placing both hands on her shoulders. I felt another glimmer of envy, watching the two friends as they consoled one another. They knew I was quiet and shy, but what they didn't know was how *alone* I really was. I had no family to fall back on, no trust funds or family dinners or shoulders to cry on...

"Rob is ... well, he's Rob. And I know you'd never do anything to intentionally hurt me. We are all in this together

... we're a team." Mia glanced over at me, waving me over to join them.

But before I could join the group hug, I heard sounds of retching from down the hall.

"Opal? Are you okay?" I peered around the corner, down the long dark hallway that led to the master bedroom. The door to the half bathroom in the hallway was ajar, but I could hear her in there, gasping for air between retching.

I walked in and found her hovered over the toilet bowl, hair plastered to the side of her face.

"You okay?"

Opal glanced up through slotted eyes, wiping her mouth with the back of her hand. I cringed at the sour smell of vomit.

"Fine," she croaked.

"You don't look fine."

Sammy and Mia had joined me in the doorway. Neither looked like they felt too sorry for Rob's new girlfriend.

"Let's get back, give her some space," I said, pulling the door closed.

Minutes later, Opal joined us in the kitchen. She looked exhausted, hair sweaty around her face, cheeks pallid.

"Feeling better?" Mia asked from her seat at the table. She had warmed up a bowl of chili. Opal glanced at the bowl, looking green.

"I think something upset my stomach last night. I was up off and on all night, throwing up." I remembered she and Rob last night, laughter tinkling from their room... *She sounded fine then*, I thought, rolling my eyes.

Opal glanced at the chili again. Mia scooped up a hearty bite, bringing it close to her lips.

"Too bad the boat has holes in it, or we could have gone to shore and picked up some antacids and crackers for you," Sammy added with a sour smile.

I cringed, watching my two friends bully Rob's girlfriend. She seemed nice enough, an outsider like me, in a way.

Opal's eyes widened as she glanced from me to Sammy. "What's wrong with the boat?" she moaned. Before we could answer, she was running back down the hall. I heard the heavy thud of the toilet seat rising and then more retches coming from her room.

Chapter Twenty-Five

Mia

I was the first to suggest we do art. It seemed insensitive, considering the skull and the boat issue, but sitting around worrying wasn't helping anything, plus the boat needed to finish drying.

First, Riley and I covered the skull with a large gray tarp from the storage building, and spread out two tarps on either side of it.

"This way, we're not interfering with a potential crime scene," I told Riley. While Riley was more than happy to help with this, and getting the easels set up in the outbuilding for me to paint, she had acted strangely about the boat this morning.

Almost like she was afraid of getting too close to it.

"Do you think someone messed with the boat?" she asked me, using heavy rocks to weigh down each corner of the tarps.

"I can't see why any of us would do that. I hope it's just bad timing, that the boat was already in disrepair before we arrived."

Riley quirked a brow at me. "I don't mean one of us did it, silly. I meant, like someone else…"

"Like who?"

"Like the guys who brought us here. Or maybe someone else?"

"Like who?" I asked again, softly. Sammy didn't like Riley, but I thought she was sweet. Naïve and awkward at times, but sweet.

"Maybe the person who did this." Riley pointed at the skull. In the light of day, it had become apparent—the skull was either real, or it was a damned good replica. Even with the skull covered, I could still feel the empty eye sockets staring back at me from underneath the tarp. Involuntarily, I shuddered. As much as I didn't want to believe, there was something eerie and unearthly about this place.

"Whoever did this did it a long time ago, though," I said, desperately.

"How do you know?" Riley asked.

My stomach clenched, eyes growing blurry as I remembered another face … another set of dead eyes staring back at me…

"There was no hair or skin attached to the skull. It's been

exposed to the elements, and I'm pretty sure it's been here a while."

"But where's the rest of it? The arms and legs ... the torso?"

I turned away from Riley, pinching my eyes closed as I took in deep breaths.

"Hey. You okay? You look like you've seen a ghost." I felt the soft brush of Riley's fingertips on my elbow. I flinched at her touch. Perhaps asking her to come do art with me was a bad idea. Working alone, and clearing my mind, was probably better.

"I'm okay, Rye. Just stressed. And to answer your question, I have no idea if someone sabotaged the boat or not. And as for the rest of the bones ... perhaps buried in the ground below the skull. I'd look closer, but I don't want to disturb the scene," I said. "I'm thinking someone was living out here."

"Maybe stuck here like we are," Riley said, breathlessly.

My chest clenched. *The boat can be repaired, can't it?*

If the others found out the truth ... they would never forgive me. *Please let the resin hold.*

Riley opened her mouth like she was about to ask another question, but I cut her off. "Let's just go work. I need to shut out everything and paint, what do you say?"

Riley's mouth spread into a hopeful grin. "I'd like to make a puzzle design for whatever you paint," she said, gleefully.

I smiled, softly. Riley was turning out to be a good friend. *Would she still like me if she knew the complete truth?*

Chapter Twenty-Six

Scarlett

"About last night..."

My brows shot up; surprised Rob was ready to discuss this so soon. I'd expected him to pretend it hadn't happened.

"Rob, we don't have to talk about it. It was a mistake, I know that... It's not a big deal."

But it is a big deal. Not only did he cheat on Opal with me, but I'd betrayed one of my best friends by kissing the guy she was still hung up on ... *and crushing my chances of getting clean while on the island.* My mind circled back to Rob's words last night... He had a connection on the mainland. How did he find someone with a hook-up so quickly, so easily?

Just ten miles away there was someone who could take all my pain and anxiety away... *I wonder if they'd come to the island and bring me some supplies, for the right price.*

"I know what we did was stupid, so can we just not do this...?" I said.

"That's not what I'm trying to say." Rob took a step closer to me; I could feel the heat rising in my cheeks as his chest brushed up against mine. He was nearly a head taller than me, and with his broad shoulders and thick, muscular arms, I felt compelled to fall into him, to let him squeeze me like a warm teddy bear...

Instead, I took a step back, smoothing my hair and glancing around nervously for the others. *If Mia catches me with the man she used to love ... still loves ... she'll kill me. Hell, the others might kill me too...*

Rob's eyes zeroed in on my lips, then he said, "I don't regret kissing you, Scarlett. I'm only sorry we didn't do more."

A flutter of desire rolled through me. I felt shivery, my hands shaking, but less from the cold and more from my arousal for him. *Why do I always go for the bad boys? It never ends well.*

"We shouldn't have kissed... Your girlfriend is here, not to mention your ex and your sister..." I tried to retort.

Rob brought his body closer to mine. I had nowhere else to go, my body pressed against the back of the house. I could feel the bulge of his erection on my belly. *There's nowhere to run to now.*

Gently, he cradled my face in his hands, rubbing the pad of his thumb softly over my lips. "I don't regret it and I want more," he said.

And there, in the light of day and completely sober, he pressed his lips to mine again.

Chapter Twenty-Seven

Sammy

The last person I expected to find my brother kissing was Scarlett. As soon as I turned the corner of the house and saw them, I leapt back, only peeking around the corner once more.

Yep. My brother and Scarlett. Damn, he sure gets around.

Irritation bloomed in my chest. I wasn't surprised by my brother's behavior—Rob was being Rob, as usual. An opportunist, always getting bored with one woman then moving on to the next.

But Scarlett. How could she do this?

For a brief moment, I considered confronting them. Marching back around the corner and smacking them both for their own stupid actions...

I'll deal with Scarlett later, I decided, turning around and scuffling over to the cottage to look for extra boat supplies. On the way, I passed the area where we had found the skull, which was covered in heavy tarps now. Our dire situation with the boat invaded my brain, and I imagined one of our own skulls tucked beneath the thin gray plastic...

We need to get off this island.

Chapter Twenty-Eight

Scarlett

The taste of Rob's lips lingered, mixed with the salt and brine of the sea. I knew I should feel guilty about the kiss, and about using drugs with him last night, but I felt heady from it, my stomach tickling, my head full of tiny balloons.

As I followed the footpath, walking alone on the island, I tried to convince myself that it was okay. Opal was nobody to me—*I don't owe any loyalty to her. And Mia ... well, supposedly she's over him, isn't she? Although we all know that is a lie.*

Riley and Mia were busy doing something in the storage building near the dock, and Sammy had gone inside, still shaken by the holes in the boat. Rob had also gone in, returning to Opal's side; she wasn't feeling well, and it bothered me a bit that he'd rushed off after our kiss to go comfort her.

I paused outside the cottage door, remembering the journal. With the boat and last night's grim discovery of the skull, I'd had very little time to read it again. *Who is Elena Blackwater? It's a catchy name—famous perhaps?* And from somewhere in the far-reaching parts of my brain, I felt like I should know it.

You know her, Scarlett. Maybe it's because you've lost too many brain cells, using when you promised you would stop...

And now, with the boat out of order, it was quite possible I would be forced to detox after all. Stuck on this tiny island long after Rob's personal supply had run dry...

The island, which had seemed gothic and vast upon arrival, now felt tiny and confining. Almost otherworldly, like we'd fallen off the map. No one was coming to save us.

What if we lie here and rot away on the island, just like that skull? What if I die like Elena did?

I considered stopping off at the cottage, taking a read and short rest, but I couldn't stop the bubble of fear in my stomach and throat. *I need to get off this island. I need to find out what happened to Elena and the owner of the mystery skull. What if they are one and the same?*

I passed the cottage, stopping at the long stretch of metal on the backside of the building. Another storage building, this one double the size of the first.

I lifted my phone camera, taking a wide shot of it. It

looked rustic and eerie, and if I applied a few filters, I could make it even creepier.

I circled the building, looking for an entrance. Disappointed to find it padlocked, I moved behind the building to get a view of the ocean water.

"Jesus." I stopped at the top of what appeared be a mountain from this angle. I stared down down, down … looking at the unforgiving drop-off below.

I never realized the island was so steep here; looking down at the crashing black waves, I estimated it was at least a 100-foot drop. Survivable, until you considered the rocks below. They looked jagged and mean, like black, rotten incisors. *Waiting to slice through my skin like butter.*

I stood at the edge, barely breathing, and I lifted my phone again to snap a pic. Vertigo hit me and I took a long step back from the edge.

Frankly, I didn't trust myself by it.

Some people are afraid of falling, but I'm more afraid of jumping.

I wasn't an unhappy person. I'd never suffered from bouts of depression or contemplated suicide … but when you're impulsive, with an addictive personality like mine, you don't always trust yourself.

I don't trust myself with Rob either.

Last night, that heady floating buzz I felt from the drug … well, it took me back to another place. Another voice: *this is the real you, not that silly try-hard who's always trying to make people like her. This is you, the real and unfiltered version.*

But that was bullshit, and I knew it.

Drugs have a way of doing that to you—making you feel like they're your best friend.

They're not.

I might let Rob kiss me again, but I won't get high anymore. I need to focus on staying clean and keeping my friends safe.

The others thought the skull was old and the boat was a fluke, but something wasn't right here... There was someone out there, planning and plotting. Watching our every move.

The more I thought about it, and the contents of that journal, the more convinced I became.

With my phone in hand, I moved back to the edge and snapped several photos of the angry, black water below. Suddenly, a branch snapped behind me and I turned, nearly losing my footing at the edge of the cliff.

There was no one there, but as I turned to look at the unforgiving rocks below ... it occurred to me where I'd heard her name.

Elena Blackwater wasn't famous. In fact, she wasn't even from Alaska.

Elena Blackwater was someone closer to home, someone I should have remembered the moment I saw the loopy black letters of her name...

Chapter Twenty-Nine

Mia

It was incredible, watching Riley work. She moved with ease, her anxiety and over-eager attitude melting away, replaced with a quiet confidence I admired.

She had drawn a schematic of the puzzle itself, and she cast the molds with a precision that felt less like art and more like science.

"Where did you learn to do this?" I asked.

"Oh." Riley stopped, removing her goggles and setting them on the workshop bench. "My father, actually."

"Are your parents still alive?" I asked. Riley was so close-lipped that I often didn't realize how little I knew about my new friend.

She shook her head. "Cancer."

"Both of them?" I asked, wide-eyed.

"Yes." She lifted the goggles, carefully placing them back on her face.

"So, your dad made puzzles? Before he died?"

"Yeah. He made all sorts of things. Puzzles, chessboards, his own boardgames. The man didn't graduate from middle school, but he was the smartest man I've ever known."

"Definitely sounds like it," I said, thoughtfully. "And he taught you?"

Riley huffed with laugher. "I wouldn't say taught. He was a quiet man, sort of like I can be, sometimes, I guess. I learned most everything from him by watching. Hours and hours, in the quiet ...watching him work his magic."

"That's incredible." I wanted to ask more, but I stayed quiet after that. Watching and learning as Riley designed the perfect puzzle cast for my painting of Whisper Island. For the first time, I realized: *I'm not the only one with parts of my past I want to keep hidden. Riley is holding something back from me too, I can feel it.*

Chapter Thirty

Riley

I t's *nerve-racking, knowing Mia Ludlow is watching me work.* She had seen me do it before, but never like this ... and never all the little details.

It's strange enough being in the same orbit as Mia, much less being friends with her.

For a moment, all of this felt normal. An everyday thing, working side by side with the most brilliant artist at Monroe ... *but there was nothing normal about this friendship.*

All of those questions about my family made me ill at ease. I'd told her my dad died of cancer, but that wasn't true. *So many parts of myself I've kept hidden from my new friends...*

"What other sort of design are you thinking? I can make

it any way you want," I said, breaking the oppressive silence in the room.

"I don't know. I just like watching your technique."

Nervously aware of Mia watching, I picked up my knife and started trimming the mold.

Chapter Thirty-One

Sammy

My blood was boiling when I entered the house. Plans of working on my digital designs were forgotten. Plans to fix up our little "paradise" house on the island, erased completely.

There was a mysterious dead person on the island, and someone had tried to sink our boat. Through the windows, I watched Scarlett as she emerged from behind the long, locked storage building. *What is she up to now?* I thought, angrily.

I should have known letting Rob come was a mistake. *If Mia finds out he's running around with Scarlett, if Opal finds out ... that could spell disaster for the group.*

But then, remembering everything else going on, and the claustrophobic fear of being stuck out here on the island for God knows how long ... Rob and Scarlett secretly messing around seemed like the least of my problems.

I wandered room to room, looking for my brother. I wanted to confront him, or at the very least urge him to not make a terrible start to our trip even worse.

"Rob?"

The door to the master bedroom was ajar. I raised my fist to knock when I heard the soft sounds of moaning. *Ugh.*

As I peeked through the crack in the door, I could see them—Opal straddling Rob, bucking forward and back. She was covered in strange, macabre tattoos.

So much for feeling sick.

I backed away from the door before they spotted me and headed for the staircase. I took the stairs two at a time, and when I was safely tucked in my room, I fell back on the bed, groaning with exasperation. I covered my head with a pillow and bit down. *Rob, you moron! Kissing one girl, then moments later... fucking another. Go figure!*

The older he got, the harder it was to justify his reckless behavior. The women and the drugs ... the constant issues with employment and money. *My brother is freaking exhausting.*

This trip was supposed to be a "vacation," but I knew from the start what it really was—a getaway. Even though I was running away from problems back home, I still didn't expect to find another stressful mess to deal with here on the island. There was so much to deal with here, too.

I took my phone out of my pocket and rolled on my

belly, before realizing I had no service. I wasn't a social media guru like Scarlett, but I'd gotten in the habit of scrolling—keeping up with the latest art trends, drama, and current world news. While, in a way, it was nice being disconnected, in another, it felt strange and scary. Being stuck out here for days, weeks, months with no way of leaving—I shivered at the thought of it.

I flicked through my old text messages, stopping at one in particular.

48 hours or I'll kill you. I'm not playing.

I held the phone to my chest and closed my eyes, fighting off the growing fear that I didn't want to accept as a possible reality. *What if they followed me to Whisper Island? What if my mistakes are the reason someone sabotaged the boat? What if the skull was a warning for me...?*

Chapter Thirty-Two

Riley

Tired from a good day's work, I joined my fellow islanders at the kitchen table for dinner. Dinner consisted of ramen and pork and beans. The others had complained a bit, but I didn't mind. I was used to eating lonely one-person meals back home in my apartment, and ramen was a staple for me growing up.

Even Opal had joined us. She was looking better after a day spent in bed, the color returning to her cheeks. Although she wasn't eating much, merely spinning noodles on her fork and watching the others.

"Wait until you see Riley's design for *The Island* puzzle. It's going to be every puzzle lover's wet dream," Mia told Scarlett, grinning.

Scarlett smiled tightly, not meeting Mia's gaze, then returned to her ramen. She'd stayed away all day. I was a little surprised when she didn't come out to see Mia's island painting, or the new die cast, but I knew she was still shaken up over discovering the skull last night.

She seemed uncharacteristically quiet tonight, keeping her head down low.

"Sounds like a great day, unless you consider our boat, and only way off this island, is filled up with water and holes," Rob said, scooping a mouthful of food in his mouth. He chewed like a cow, his jaw grinding, exposing a mouthful of mush.

Mia gave him a dark look. "The boat will be fine. We'll check on the resin tomorrow, see if it's dried. And regardless, you guys, more boats will come by or Juan and the others will return to check on us soon. We have plenty of supplies here until we can get in contact with the cops."

Truthfully, I didn't remember Juan or the others saying they would return. *Did he tell Mia that when I wasn't around?* I wondered.

I remembered Juan promising to transport Rob to the island when he arrived on the mainland. But Rob had beaten us to the island, showing up all on his own...

"Who brought you and Opal to the island?" I asked, directing my question to Opal with a polite smile.

"Oh." She bunched up her brows, in thought. "I don't remember their names. Do you, Rob?"

"Two guys at the marina. I paid them fifty bucks to bring

us over early. Didn't want to waste money on a hotel, waiting for you ladies to arrive." Rob was looking at Scarlett strangely, but she kept her head down, shoveling bites in her mouth like she was eating out of a trough. *She's really out of it tonight… What is she hiding?*

Opal cleared her throat, breaking Rob's gaze. "So, I know I was not much help today with my stomach bug, but I was thinking about the boat. I know it seems like a simple solution, but have you all considered duct tape? My dad used to say that's there nothing duct tape can't fix."

Mia snickered, rolling her eyes at Opal. Opal narrowed her eyes back, angrily.

"No, she's right," Sammy said. "It's unlikely that the resin will hold since the boat was wet when it was applied, and there are so many additional small holes to contend with." She side-eyed her brother. "If we plugged the holes, then sealed them tightly with duct tape, we could test it out near the island to make sure it works before we try to take it all the way back to shore."

My stomach did a somersault, thinking about depending on a boat full of holes sealed by duct tape getting me safely back to shore.

"What if it doesn't work?" I asked the obvious question.

Opal, looking pleased with Sammy's support, said, "Well, we will have life jackets, of course. And we'll have to test it out to make sure first, like she said. I'm not an artist like you girls, but I'm pretty handy and I'll make sure it's good and sealed, I promise."

"We need to get off this island." Scarlett raised her voice, finally looking back at us. One by one, she looked at each one of us.

"We'll be okay, Scarlett..." Sammy put a hand on Scarlett's shoulder, but she quickly brushed her off.

"We won't if we stay here. I can feel it, deep in my bones. Someone is out there, waiting and watching. Someone did this to the boat on purpose."

Mia cleared her throat and stood up. "I can't take any more of this negativity. I'm going to bed," she announced. Scarlett's eyes never left Mia, watching her as she carried bowls to the sink and dropped them in with a clatter.

We all watched Mia sulk off from the kitchen, then listened to the angry slaps of her feet running up the stairs.

"Have you been smoking something, Scarlett? Snorting something? Because you're not acting like yourself at all today. I mean, I know we're all stressed, but I don't think anyone is going to hurt us. Safety in numbers, right?" Sammy nudged her, a little too hard.

I expected Scarlett to get defensive at Sammy's suggestion—that she was high on something and overreacting—but she just shook her head, finishing her last bit of noodles.

"There's only safety in numbers if those numbers are on your side," Scarlett said. We watched her exit the kitchen, leaving her bowl behind on the table.

"Weird," Sammy said, shaking her head.

"And rude," Opal huffed, picking up Scarlett's dirty bowl and taking it to the sink.

"I'm going to bed. Worn out from today," I said awkwardly, excusing myself. I ran upstairs, hoping to catch Mia alone before she closed herself in her room for the night.

Chapter Thirty-Three

Mia

I picked up my pile of sketches, flipping through them but not really seeing them, then tossed them back on the floor beside the bed. It was nearly midnight, and once again, the house was shrouded in eerie silence. I'd been unable to fall asleep, working on some new ideas to distract me. I was happy with my island painting from this afternoon, but tonight's work had all been duds.

The fact was: Rob's being here was throwing me off. Opal was lovely and annoying, and I absolutely hated her. Just seeing them together ... her wrapping her arms around his waist in the kitchen, her batting her eyes, her stupid big ring and her stupid tattoo ... and her clinging to every word he said... *Disgusting.*

Opal's behavior bothered me because once upon a time,

I'd been the same way. Enamored with Rob, magnetized by his charm. Convinced he was honest about his feelings for me.

Rob has this way of making you feel like you're the only girl in the room, at least he used to…

A memory snaked in—Rob, cupping my chin in his hands. Rob, smoothing a wayward hair behind my ear. Rob, whispering a slew of promises, saying those three little words every woman wants to hear from time to time…

But seeing him with Opal tonight, and even the strange way Scarlett watched him … made me realize how immune other women were to his phony ways, made me humiliated remembering my own actions. I could remember asking him—*begging him*—to stay. Calling and texting, following him to bars and hangouts I knew he would be at. Anything to gain back his love and affection.

One day I was the center of his world and the next day I'd fallen off the edge of it—Rob was self-centered and impulsive like that. He fell hard, and he fell out harder.

I'd told him so many things about myself, given up private pieces of me … and I thought he knew me enough to at least be honest when his feelings changed.

It's a good thing we ended things when we did.

Now, I only wished that Sammy hadn't let him come. She told me that she had no choice, that she was in trouble back home, but she hadn't given me all the details yet. *Is it possible she's just making up excuses, lying so I won't be mad?* I wondered. I, too, hadn't discussed the recent articles and fears over the anniversary of my mistakes ... but still.

Maybe she just made up the part about being in danger to help me swallow Rob's presence here, without question.

No, Sammy wouldn't do that. She's many things, but she's never been a liar.

Giving up on sleep, I crept out of bed. The house was chilly, settling deep in my bones. I tugged on an oversized sweatshirt that was covered in paint stains. In the low-lit room, I stared at myself in the mirror. I knew I was pretty, but I wasn't one of THOSE girls. I didn't know the first thing about fashion, choosing clothes that were comfortable or functional instead, and I wore very little makeup.

Wispy curls of hair poked out from my ponytail. With a huff, I tried to blow them out of my face. *Maybe if I were more put together like Opal or Scarlett, Rob wouldn't have left me. I never understood what he saw in me in the first place.*

My stomach gurgled, reminding me that I'd skipped lunch and ate truly little for dinner. As I tiptoed through the hallway, my stomach roiled noisily again. Deciding to warm up a bowl of chili, I descended the stairs, stepping carefully on each cold, wooden step in the dark.

My mind was focused on food as I reached the bottom of the stairs. As I crossed the living room, I was met by the smell of smoke.

"What the hell?"

I stormed through the living room hallway, running for the kitchen. Heavy black smoke rose from the sink.

Covering my mouth, I approached the sink. A pot sat in the center of the deep sink basin, rolling with fire.

Frantic, I reached for a towel on the counter and flipped the faucet on, trying to fan the flames and extinguish the fire. But the more I tried, the higher the flames rose.

"Shit, shit, shit…"

Somewhere in the deep recesses of my brain, I remembered my father's words: "Never put water on a grease fire." *What if it's grease in the pot that's caught fire?*

Stricken with fear, I shouted for the others while I ransacked the cabinets, looking for baking soda. Gagging on the thick black smoke filling my lungs, I cried out in relief as I wrapped my hands around a packet of flour.

I ripped the pack open, flour bursting through the air, and I dumped all of it into the sink. Immediately, the fire began to die down. I used a hand towel to swat at the remaining flames.

Breathless, I looked up to see Opal standing in the kitchen doorway, droopy-eyed and dazed. "What's going on?" she asked, sleepily. *What's going on? Seriously?*

Heavy thumps rang out, as my friends came barreling down the stairs. Riley and Sammy raced to my side.

"What happened, Mia?" Sammy's eyes were wide with fright. She looked around at all the flour and smoke, then leaned over to peer in the sink.

"There was a fire. I put it out," I gasped. My hands were shaking uncontrollably as I wobbled over to the kitchen table and pulled out a seat.

Riley started to turn on the faucet.

"Don't," I warned, "it's grease. I used flour to put it out."

Opal moved to the kitchen window, struggling to get the rusty latch unlocked. "We need some air in here. I can't breathe," she moaned.

Riley was still bent over the sink. "It's definitely grease," she said, "and this." Through pinched fingers, she held up a black, shriveled ball.

"What is that?"

Riley sniffed it. "Looks like a rag that was soaked in grease or something. Was someone in here cooking?"

Sammy raised her eyebrows, looking around the room. "Good question. Did you see anyone in here when you came down, Mia?"

I shook my head. "I couldn't sleep so I came down to get a snack. I smelled smoke as soon as I reached the foot of the stairs."

"I'm surprised you didn't smell it, Opal," Riley said. For someone who was usually so kind and soft-spoken, there was a sharp edge to her voice.

Opal looked sheepish. "I sleep like the dead. Plus, I've been sick all day, remember?"

"I'm just glad I came in in time," I said, rubbing my sooty hands on my soft pajama pants. Suddenly, I was feeling very tired, ready to curl up in bed and sleep for ten hours.

"Well, this fire couldn't have started itself," Riley

muttered, wincing as she tried to lift the pan from the sink and dropped it. From here, I could see ugly black marks scorching the once-white marble.

"Where's my brother?" Sammy asked, turning to Opal.

Opal, still dazed, looked around the room as though she were expecting Rob to materialize from thin air. "I don't know. He wasn't in bed when I jumped up. I heard Mia screaming so I ran..."

"And Scarlett's not here either," I said, worriedly.

Chapter Thirty-Four

Sammy

I shouted my brother's name in the wind, jogging down the footpath in the dark. The first storage building had been empty, no sounds or signs of Rob.

Opal and Mia were back at the house, searching. I let out a painful cry as Riley stepped on the back of my heel.

"Watch where you're going!" I snapped over my shoulder like a wild animal.

Riley flinched. Stopped in her tracks.

I stopped too. "Look, I'm sorry. I'm scared, okay? Why don't we split up? You look over by the dock area and I'll check out the cottage and other building on the island."

"I-I'm not sure if that's a good idea. What if there's someone out here?" Riley asked. "Whoever set that fire…"

"Fine! Just don't walk all over me, please." I charged

forward on the path, cupping my hands around my mouth and yelling for Rob.

"We should probably yell for Scarlett, too," Riley said.

I was glad it was dark so she couldn't see me roll my eyes. "Fine. Do whatever you want," I said.

We were nearing the cottage and the makeshift tarp grave when I heard someone sobbing up ahead.

"Rob!" Running now, I screamed my brother's name, following the muffled cries.

My foot caught the edge of a knotted root. I fell full-length, catching my fall painfully with my elbows, making a strangled "oof" sound. Riley grasped me from behind, pulling me onto my feet, surprising me with her physical strength.

"Rob, where are you?" Riley shouted. She put up a finger, silencing me, as I dusted off my shirt and leggings. She was right; in the surrounding quiet, I could hear the muffled sobs from before.

"That's definitely him," I said, stiffening. "But why isn't he answering us?"

Riley veered off the path, twisting through the trees, and this time, it was me staying on her heels.

"Over there."

I gasped when I saw him, covering my mouth and nose.

He was bent over on the ground like a wounded beast, shoulders hunched and shaking. His face buried in his hands.

"Rob…"

He didn't turn around when I said his name. But as I drew closer, I saw what lay beneath him on the ground. A tangle of bright red hair, fiery even in the velvety night sky.

Scarlett's eyes were wide, unblinking. She lay on her back, hands curled into strange talons at her side.

Her abdomen was split wide open.

Chapter Thirty-Five

Riley

S ammy's screams ripped the air, her pain and agony rocking me off my feet. I landed on my knees beside Scarlett's dead body, taking in the gaping red wound and stony, fearful expression on her cold, white face. *This certainly wasn't an accident.*

"What the hell happened?"

Rob was shaking, his face moon white in the dark. He looked at me, registering my presence for the first time.

"Was it an animal?" I asked, even though I knew the answer. *Wounds that precise don't come from animals and animals don't leave that much flesh behind.*

Rob shook his head back and forth, back and forth ... then erupted into sobs again. Sammy, getting a hold of herself at the sight of her brother's weeping, wrapped her arms around his shoulders.

Rob closed his eyes, leaning into his sister's embrace. I was reminded, then, how new to the group I truly was—I didn't know what to say or do that might provide comfort.

"What the hell happened, Rob? What happened to Scarlett? Please tell us," Sammy said, rubbing his back and arm in slow, soothing circles.

I watched the two of them, seeing the true closeness of their bond for the first time. Sammy's embrace was like a mother's, protective and immovable. *There was something so strange about it ... unhealthy.* My own father avoided physical contact at all costs. *Probably not healthy either.*

"I-I was supposed to meet her. She told me to be here at midnight," Rob said. But there was more to it than that, a guilty glint in his eye. *Scarlett and Rob really were hooking up on the island, just as I suspected earlier.*

"Why were you supposed to meet her?" I asked, just as Sammy narrowed her eyes at me.

"Is that really important right now?" Sammy went back to rubbing her brother's head and shoulders, trying to calm him down. "Tell us what happened, Rob," she said, her voice soft and buttery sweet.

"I was running late. It took Opal forever to fall asleep, so I made some homemade gravy—I thought it'd be nice for us to have some in the morning for breakfast..."

I thought about the burning pot in the sink. *What an irresponsible jerk!*

"I looked at my watch and it was quarter past twelve. That's when I remembered I was meeting Scarlett." Rob glanced over his shoulder at Scarlett now, bloody and lifeless on the ground. Another gasping sob racked through him.

Sammy clutched him in her arms, as though he were the one who just got murdered. I turned my attention back to Scarlett, staring at the vicious wound on her belly.

"Whoever did this was furious," I whispered, my body quivering. "Someone who wanted to hurt her. Someone who wanted us to find her here ... as a warning."

"You think?" Sammy said, practically snarling at me. In that moment, I hated her. *Why is she always so mean to me?*

Ignoring her rudeness, I said, "Was she like this when you got here, or...?"

Sammy huffed. "Or what? You think my brother did this?"

"I'm not saying that," I said, raising my own voice this time. "I just want to know what happened to my friend."

My friend. The memories played like an old movie reel— *Scarlett introducing herself on that first day in class. Scarlett taking me to meet her friends. Scarlett drinking and laughing, her beautiful rose-red lips and hair ... her infectious sense of humor. She filled a room without even speaking, that's how big and bright her personality was. But then there were the drugs and darkness —secrets she tried, unsuccessfully, to keep.*

"She was like this when I found her," Rob whimpered in confirmation.

Sammy's eyes softened as she stared past her brother at her friend's dead body.

"She told us we were in danger and we didn't listen." It was Mia's voice now, barely a whisper behind me. She crumpled to the ground and I tried to catch her, but it was too late.

"If she was like this when he got here ... and all of us were inside, then that can only mean one thing," Mia said, eyes lifting to meet mine.

I nodded, solemnly.

"There's someone else on the island with us. Someone who wants us dead," I told them.

Chapter Thirty-Six

Opal

I never wanted to come here in the first place. I don't like planes and I don't like boats. And I don't like cold places, like Alaska. And I certainly don't like being stranded on an island with some sort of psychopath.

But Rob begged me. Well, I wouldn't necessarily say begged—he asked sweetly, purring in my ear, trying to convince me he'd be lonely without me.

It wasn't until we were halfway here that he told me about his ex. I'd heard him talk about Mia before, but I had no idea she was roommates with his sister. And I certainly didn't know she was coming to the island.

Standing here now, legs shaking in my boots, I watch my boyfriend as he sobs into his sister's arms.

Riley tried to nudge me forward, but my feet stayed frozen on the footpath.

We had heard the screams, shrill and painful, almost like the call of a wild, helpless animal in the dark. Mia and I had raced through the rickety house and through the trees, heading for the sounds coming from Sammy.

The redhead, Scarlett, was lying dead on the ground. I listened to Rob explain to his sister and that weird girl Riley about how he was supposed to meet up with Scarlett.

A girl has been murdered. That's all that should have mattered. But all I could see, and feel, was red-hot rage running through my veins. *It took Opal forever to fall asleep—*Rob's words ricocheted through my skull like ping-pong balls, painful and abrupt.

That's why he kept trying to rush me to bed. He wanted to sneak off and meet that bitch Scarlett. Only been here a couple days, and he's already grown tired of me! What an asshole!

I watched Mia, with her unkempt hair and reckless beauty, as she crawled around Rob and Sammy so she could see her friend. For the first time, I felt a kinship toward her—she, too, had been hurt by Rob. We'd both fallen for his bullshit.

"Oh, Scarlett. I'm so sorry," Mia moaned. She leaned over her friend, and for a moment, I thought she was going to kiss her. But it sounded like she was whispering in the dead girl's ear. Tears trickled down her face.

Still unable to move, I stared at the dark nasty wounds on Scarlett's abdomen. Undoubtedly, they were caused by a knife, or another similar, sharp tool. Not an animal, like that moron Riley suggested.

"We need to get back to the house right now," I said, voice rising.

Sammy and Rob turned their heads, seeing me standing behind them for the first time.

"She's right," Riley said. "There's someone out here. Someone did this to Scarlett and right now, we need to get inside and secure the windows and doors. When the sun comes up, we'll do whatever it takes to repair the boat and get to shore so we can bring in the cops."

"But … what about her?" Rob pointed at Scarlett.

The red-hot rage was back. *A girl was murdered, and I shouldn't be focused on my cheating boyfriend*, I reminded myself. *But if I had a knife, I'd murder Rob right now too.*

"We can't just leave her lying there … not like that," Rob whined.

As though he even knew the girl. They just met like twenty-four hours ago, I thought.

"I'll get another tarp," Sammy said, releasing her hold on Rob and getting back on her feet. "Nobody wants to leave her out here, but we can't move her. That might destroy evidence. The best we can do is grab some tarps from the equipment building and cover her up until morning."

One by one, we filed down the footpath, leaving the dead girl behind.

I looked left to right as we trudged down the path,

looking for movement through the trees. *Someone is here on the island with us. Someone who wants us dead. If not ... the only alternative was that Scarlett's killer was among us. Perhaps one of us...*

Chapter Thirty-Seven

Mia

"Who do you think they were?" I pointed at one of the photographs with a shaky finger. A young mother and father, two sweet little girls. They looked so happy in their family photos.

"I don't know, and I don't care. I just want off this fucking island," Opal huffed, from where she was curled up on the couch, still shivering.

I flinched at the harshness of her words, teeth grinding in anger, but then I chose to ignore it. All that mattered right now was getting justice for Scarlett and keeping the rest of my friends safe through the night.

We were all huddled together in the living room, two candles burning dimly. Rob and Sammy sat together on the loveseat; Sammy looked numb, whereas Rob's face still twisted with anguish. *He barely knew Scarlett. Why does he get to be so upset?* I thought, cruelly. But then I brushed that off. We'd all lost her, and every one of us had a right to be afraid right now.

Sammy and Rob had been through a lot with their parents. Rob was prone to depression and anxiety when stressed. He was still shaking and teary-eyed, and I looked away as Sammy tried to console him.

I hate that I know so much about him. And I hate that I care so much. Why did I ever agree to come to this Godforsaken place?

I closed my eyes, remembering another time … another dead girl's face. Shuddering, I turned away from my friends so they wouldn't see my anguish.

I wondered, not for the first time, why Rob and Scarlett were meeting up so late. I could only guess that it was for obvious reasons: some sort of late-night hook-up. My friend was gone, and no matter how badly it hurt that she was trying to hook up with Rob, none of that mattered now. I'd kindly throw him in the sea, but Scarlett … her life had mattered more to me. *She was the pinnacle of our group, the anchor that kept us all connected … and now she's gone.*

Riley and Opal were on the sofa, sitting at opposite ends from each other. Opal stared down at her hands, opening and closing her tiny fists, and Riley sat with her knees tucked against her chest, chin resting on top as she shook with anxiety.

"Are you sure we got everything locked?" Riley said, scanning the room.

"Pretty sure," I said, honestly.

After we had covered Scarlett with a blue plastic tarp, we had gone room to room, securing every door and window in the house. I had also taken out a sharp knife from the drawer in the kitchen and placed it on the mantel. *Just in case.*

"Are you sure you didn't see anyone else out there?" I asked Rob, not for the first time.

He shook his head at me, eyes lingering on mine for several seconds.

"No one on the footpath, no sounds from the cottage or that other locked building?" I pressed.

"No. Nothing."

"That building—what if someone is hiding out in there? There was a padlock on it, but maybe we could break it open. Confront whoever did this," Riley said, suddenly acting brave even though moments ago she looked like a deer in headlights.

"We need to leave that up to the police. No one is going out there tonight," I sighed.

"You're right. It was just a thought... Seems strange that it's the only place locked up on the entire island," Riley said.

"We need to get some sleep," Opal groaned. I raised a brow at her.

"You really think any of us are going to be able to sleep with our friend murdered in cold blood out there?" Sammy scoffed.

Opal's face softened. "I know it will be hard. But I think we should leave at first light, and we should all leave together. Safety in numbers."

There it was again—*safety in numbers.* I looked around the room, shadows dancing in the candlelight, casting my friends' faces into eerie, orange, ghoulish masks.

Does someone in this room have a motive for hurting Scarlett? I wondered, the thought springing up from nowhere.

Rob was nearby when it happened; if Opal had caught them together, flipped out because she was jealous…

No. No, none of these people were capable of killing Scarlett. Were they?

"I'll tape up the boat and we'll make sure it's safe enough to get to shore tomorrow. I know I can fix it," Opal said.

"Opal is right, you guys. We need to rest. Daylight is still seven hours away and we'll need all our strength to get off this island and get the help we need. We might have to paddle all the way to shore if the motor acts up," I said, solemnly.

Rob and Sammy grunted "okay" in unison.

"Our rooms have locks on them. We should sleep in pairs and each take a knife with us, to protect ourselves just in case. If whoever wanted us dead wasn't a coward, they would have already broken in here by now. I'm quite sure they're hiding out there in the dark, and they only hurt Scarlett because she was all alone," Sammy said, talking through her teeth. Rob's face fell at the mention of

Scarlett again. He obviously felt bad for showing up late for the late-night hook-up session. Not to mention practically burning the house down with his irresponsible late-night cooking. As awful as he could be sometimes, I couldn't see him hurting a woman. Or anyone, for that matter...

I tried not to think about Scarlett out there, all alone; tried to focus on my love for my friend, instead of how she looked ... tried not to think about the deep, dark wounds on her belly. Or the anger it took to inflict them. *The evil it required...*

There was a time in my life when I thought I was evil. Hell, most of the people who remember my freshman year at Monroe would probably agree.

"I guess ... you and I could bunk together in my room," Riley suggested, looking at me.

"That's fine. Your bed is bigger anyway," I agreed.

"I'm sleeping alone," Opal said, raising her chin.

"No way," I said. "We all need to stay in pairs until morning..."

"I'll be fine. I'd rather sleep alone than bunk with him." She jerked a thumb over at Rob.

He grimaced.

"He can stay in my room," Sammy said, patting her brother on the back. Something about the two of them was making me feel physically ill. What were they hiding? It was Rob's friend who owned this place... *What do we really know about him?* And, once again, I remembered Sammy's dire face that night at Molly's Motel, as she mentioned trouble back home...

"I'm staying alone," Opal repeated, looking around the room. Daring any of us to challenge her.

Although I didn't agree with Opal's decision, I had to respect it. *I'd rather be alone than with an asshole like Rob right now, too.*

Chapter Thirty-Eight

Sammy

My body thick with tension and fear, I shoved the covers back on the queen bed and motioned for my brother to climb in beside me. He was pacing, wringing his hands uncontrollably like he used to do when we were kids, and for a moment, I thought he might refuse to get in.

But then, his hands dropped to his sides and I watched his body unfold, collapsing in the bed beside me. He covered his face with his hands, rubbing them up and down, then back and forth. It almost felt like old times, just me and him against the world. We rarely talked about our parents—the roaches and the unpaid bills... Worst of all there were the cruel words and the hitting, then all the horrible stints in foster care. When our parents died in a drunk driving accident, I didn't cry for them. I consoled

Rob and promised to take care of him as long as I lived. I swallowed the pain so I could bear the brunt of his, simple as that.

"Stop that." I rolled onto my side and tugged his hands away from his face. He was rubbing at his cheeks so harshly, he was bound to take some skin off them.

I looked my brother in the eyes, realization seeping in. *He's high. I can't believe I didn't see it earlier. He must have brought drugs to the island.*

And as much as I wanted to confront him, now was not the time to do it. We had to get off this island. I wasn't sure if what happened to Scarlett had to do with me—*how could they possibly find me here?* But I wasn't expelling the idea. I'd pissed off my boss enough that he wanted to kill me.

"Talk to me, Rob. Are you okay?"

"Okay? Of course, I'm not fucking okay. Are you? It's your friend out there dead on the island. She's all alone ... all cut up like that..."

I propped myself up with my elbow, jaw flexing with anger. Leave it to Rob to make this all about him.

"Exactly, Rob. She was *my* friend. And it's fucked up, all right? I guess I'm still kind of in shock about it. It doesn't feel real—none of this does."

Rob's pained expression softened. He looked at me, really looked, as though he were seeing me for the first time since I'd arrived on the island.

"I'm sorry, sis. I know you're hurting. But I promise you

that I'll kill the bastard who did this to Scarlett. I will, I swear…"

I shushed him with a finger. "We'll let the cops handle it tomorrow. I'm more convinced than ever that there's someone out there—someone roaming around the island, watching us through the trees."

Rob looked toward the closed second-story window as though he might catch a glimpse of this phantom menace in the trees beyond.

"Tell me everything you know about this place," I pressed him. "You mentioned your friend Manny told you about the island. His family owned it. How much do you know about him or his background?"

Rob's eyes skimmed the ceiling, as though the answer to this mystery were embedded in its swirly popcorn patterns. Finally, he said, "Well, I know Manny pretty well, I guess. We worked at the car wash together."

"The car wash?" I racked my brain, flashing through the dozens of failed jobs Rob had held over the past decade. I wondered if this Manny was less of a friend and more of a drug connection. Suddenly, I wanted to kick myself for not asking more questions about the island itself and the people who had lived here before.

"Yeah. We haven't hung out in a few years though. We mostly keep in touch through social media. That's how it is for everyone these days, isn't it?"

Confused, I lifted myself to a sitting position. "If you

haven't seen him in years, how did the whole island thing come up?"

"He sent me a message with the pictures of it. When I rambled on and on about what a lucky little dick he was for having his own island, he offered to let us come stay here any time. We talked a couple times after that. I mean, he knew we were coming to the island, but we didn't really discuss details about the island itself."

"Whoa, Rob. This is a little too fucking shady, even for you. You're not serious, are you? You all never actually spoke?"

Rob groaned. "Why do you always have to mother me, huh? I'm the oldest, remember?"

"Then act like it," I growled.

"We discussed it in the messages, okay? He said I could come whenever I wanted. And if you're implying that Manny is some crazed killer out here on the island ... well, that's stupid as fuck, Sammy. He's back home in Tennessee. He's my friend, and a good one. He told me that he had no use for this place, and he was having trouble selling it. Said it made no difference to him if I came out here or not ... that he wasn't using it, so I might as well..."

How convenient. At a time when I needed to get away—and get away fast—Rob's old friend pops up on social media, letting him borrow an exclusive island on the other side of the world. Something isn't right here. Something that sounds too good to be true usually is...

"I'll call him when we get to the mainland, all right? We

will go to the cops and tell them about Scarlett. Then I'll call Manny and tell him, too. After that, we are getting the fuck out of Alaska and never looking back," Rob said.

But the last thing I needed was contact with the police, and there was no way I could go home either. Not with all the trouble I was in. Hell, for all I knew, there was already a warrant out for my arrest... Hell, going to jail might be my best bet if whoever killed Scarlett really had me in mind as their target.

But then my mind flashed back to Scarlett ... the deep, crimson wounds in her stomach. Those cruel, angry slashes on her beautiful skin...

"What were you doing out there with her anyway, Rob?" *As though I don't already know the answer.*

Rob rolled over, facing me. His eyes were pupil-less in the dark.

"I liked her, okay? She seemed cool. And we ... sort of hit it off yesterday."

Not for the first time, I wanted to reach out and smack my brother. How could someone his age act so impulsively?

"So, let me get this straight. You're on a deserted island with your new girlfriend and your old girlfriend, and you couldn't resist going after another girl?"

"Fuck off, Sammy. It wasn't like that."

"Then what was it like? Do tell! Or wait... I know. She was different, yeah? You thought that maybe she was the one ... blah blah blah. I've heard it all before with you. Another broken fucking record. And, by the way, I know you're using too. What is it this time? Pills again? Or have you graduated to shooting up, huh?"

"You know what? Fuck you. I'd rather go beg for Opal's forgiveness than sit and listen to this shit."

I refused to look at my brother as he stomped around the room, gathering up his robe and other belongings. I thought about stopping him, but I was so angry—and so upset about my friend and disappointed in him—that I couldn't do it.

He slammed the door on his way out. The windows rattled in their panes like a distant warning and suddenly, I was alone in the dark again.

Chapter Thirty-Nine

Rob

A s I lifted my fist to knock on Opal's door, I could literally *feel* her anger and fury penetrating through the thick wood frame. *Every single woman in this house hates me.*

Opal had overheard me outside, admitting to a planned meet-up with Scarlett before I found her dead. And she knows me well enough to know that it wasn't going to be something nice and friendly.

This isn't the first time I've cheated on Opal. And we've only been together for a few months.

Turning from the door, I wandered into the kitchen instead, feeling my way along and flipping on lights. The kitchen smelled like burnt plastic and I wrinkled my nose at the messy black pan that I'd used earlier in the sink. *What the hell happened in here?* I wondered.

My stomach turned, not from hunger or from finding a dead body or from fear … no, my body wanted something different. I couldn't smoke fentanyl in the house; I'd have to do it outside where no one else could see or smell it.

Quietly, I went to the front door. I unlocked the deadbolt and cracked the door, peeping out for monsters in the dark. *I won't go far. Just down by the dock, where I can quickly run for the front door if I see anyone.*

My cheeks burned with shame. *I shouldn't be running from anyone. I should be the man here, protecting these women from this faceless villain on the island. I should have been able to protect Scarlett. If I hadn't been late to meet her, would she still be alive?*

Impulsively, I flung the door open and marched toward the trees. The thought of lighting up, the taste on the back of my tongue … made it worth the risk.

Scarlett had been worth the risk too, I decided, pressing my back to a tree as I dug around in my right jeans pocket for the dope.

Sammy and I were alike in some ways, but whereas she dealt with the death of our parents by focusing on her digital artwork and overachieving and controlling every aspect of our lives … I went the opposite direction.

It's like there's this gaping black hole inside me. No matter how hard I try to fill it up, nothing works. I get these ideas …

these plans. But then they're all fleeting, my interest lost the moment I get close to achieving them...

Take Mia for instance. I was obsessed with her. My sister's roommate, the daughter of a famous artist with a dark, troubled past... She was drop-dead gorgeous, but not in that classic way some girls are. No, Mia wore her beauty like a careless scarf, an afterthought. It was her mind that drove me crazy.

And maybe that's why I had to end things. She was too good, too much. I didn't want to have to work that hard to keep her.

Other girls were easier... I liked them fast and loose on the weekends, but then I'd find another good one and fuck it all up again. Like I did with Opal.

Scarlett felt different. There was something ugly about her. Deep inside, like my ugly could feel hers too. And she liked getting high—which was something Mia and Opal would never do.

When Scarlett and I made plans to meet up, it was to smoke. As much as we wanted each other sexually, we also wanted that rush of getting high too.

Because of me Scarlett gave up her sobriety. Because of me Scarlett is dead.

I tried to push away thoughts of her face ... those perky red lips and that wild hair... It's too bad she's dead. *Despite Sammy's teasing, Scarlett really might have been the one ... you never know.*

I tried, again and again, to light the end of my pipe. But the wind felt like a squall was coming; as it whispered through the trees, I could taste salt on my lips. For the first time, I realized why it was called Whisper Island.

Waves crashed against the rocks, cruel and unforgiving. Once again, I tried to light my pipe, bending my head down low. But to no avail.

I had no choice but to move away from the wind, deeper through the trees.

But then I saw something out of the corner of my eye. Something dark, something growing … getting bigger.

"Who's there?" I took two steps forward, my foot catching on a gnarly root. As I stumbled, my pipe went sailing through the air.

"Shit shit shit!" The whispering shadows forgotten, I fell to my knees. Crawling through the dark, painful roots, trying to find my dope.

I'd left my cell phone behind in Sammy's room. There was no reception out here, but I could have used it for light. *Dammit! I need that pipe!*

A twig snapped nearby and branches shuffled behind me. I stopped moving, flesh crawling with fear.

Slowly, I lifted my face. Shadows danced through the trees. That's when I saw it: a masked face peering back at me, a wild grin in the dark.

I opened my mouth. Screamed as loud as I could.

My screams. Surely someone will hear them and come running.

But then the wind swallowed my cries and I felt cold steel as it connected with the back of my head.

Chapter Forty

Opal

The joke was on them, pairing up in those creaky old beds, gifting me with the biggest room all to myself. The bed was king-sized and sturdy. I tried not to think about the scratchy blankets, Rob making love to me only hours earlier ... *ugh*.

The claw-foot tub was the best part of the entire house, in my opinion. As I filled the ceramic tub with steaming hot water and bubbles, I tried not to think about how it should be Rob and I in it together. Not me, by myself, sulking.

I was stupid to think he was different. That I was the one who could change him.

I'd known Rob for months before we started dating; I made the pizzas and he delivered them. Our daily exchanges were fun and flirtatious, but I knew—*I knew*

215

—that those exchanges were not unique. Rob flirted with the cashier and other drivers. He even flirted with our boss and the lady who dropped off our mail.

Rob had this way about him—this way of making you feel that when he looked at you, you were the only one alive in the room. His stare was intense, mischievous. *He's undressing you with his eyes,* my co-workers liked to tease when he came in.

And then it happened—one night, he asked me out on a proper date. We weren't supposed to date our co-workers, even though we rarely worked side by side, so, at first, we had to keep it a secret.

We went out that first night and I slept with him right off the bat. And the next time we did it again. And the next time and the next … until, finally, weeks had turned into months and we were inseparable.

I thought he would change, though. I didn't think he'd keep flirting, keep teasing the other girls. *That's just my personality, Ope. You know that,* Rob would say.

But the part of his personality that attracted me in the beginning made me want to kill him in the end. After I found out he got drunk and slept with someone else at a party (*It meant nothing, I promise, Ope!* he had claimed), that should have been the end of it.

But I forgave him, and that adrenaline rush he gave me in the beginning came rushing back… *He's mine. This time I'm going to keep him all to myself,* I had thought.

And when he invited me to the island, I couldn't hide

my surprise. It felt serious—taking me on a vacation, where I would finally get to meet his sister who he thought of as a second mom.

But then, as I learned on the flight, it wasn't just Sammy I would be meeting. Mia, the famous artist and the only girl who ever made Rob weepy-eyed and serious when he brought her up, would also be coming. Scarlett was a wild card. I didn't expect her to be the one I had to worry about...

But now she's dead.

And as terrible as that is ... maybe karma really does exist. She shouldn't have been messing with another girl's boyfriend. The others would never say that, but I will. Scarlett got exactly what she deserved.

I had only just submerged myself in the water when I heard the undeniable creak of footsteps coming down the hall. I froze, holding my breath and covering my chest as I strained to hear who was coming. *Did I lock the bedroom door? Suddenly, I couldn't remember.*

Quietly, I lifted myself from the tub, let the sudsy bubbles drip over my naked body, streaking my tattooed legs. The thought of Rob coming in, finding me wet and naked like this, and begging for my forgiveness ... gave me an ache of desire.

I stood still, listening. Trying not to consider the other alternative—an angry murderer, wielding a knife, coming to split me open just like he did to that bitch Scarlett...

"Rob? Is that you?" I stepped over the side of the tub,

reaching desperately for my towel that hung over the bar. But the moment my left foot touched the slick white tiles below, it slipped out from under me. I went down sideways, my left hipbone and elbow connecting with the cold, hard floor below.

"Uhhh…" I moaned, the pain so sharp and brutal, that I could barely breathe. *Stupid. Stupid. Stupid. Why didn't I put down a towel before getting in?*

Wincing, I rolled onto all fours.

I heard the bedroom door click shut.

"Rob?" Humiliated for him to see me like this, I crawled for the bathroom door, eager to slam it shut until I could stand up and at least get a towel around me.

But two heavy black boots filled the doorway. I looked up, following the legs all the way to the waist, and on up to the face. They were wearing a ski mask, face completely covered but for their eyes and mouth. It was hard to see at first, but then a flicker of recognition sparked in my brain— *I'd know those eyes anywhere.*

Day Three

Chapter Forty-One

Riley

I n the early morning light, the house had a sound all its own. Walls groaned, floors creaked, and wind whispered through the cracks in the window glass, creating an oddly calming orchestra of sound.

Whisper Island, the silence here is loud sometimes…

Mia was purring in the bed beside me, each breath blowing wispy, careless bangs from her face.

The events of the night before came rushing back… Scarlett, the rose-red slash on her belly… Her eyes, so wide and *dead*, staring blankly back up at me.

"Do you really think an animal could have done that?" Mia's voice vibrated my cheek. I shivered, despite myself. When I looked over, her eyes were tiny slits, watching me in the dusty stream of morning light.

It's almost like we're connected, our brains passing back and forth information... It was a strange thought, but one I couldn't seem to shake for several moments. I came to the island so I could get closer to the girls, but specifically, closer to Mia. It was she who I felt the most connected to, the one whose trust I needed to earn.

"I don't know. It's possible, I guess..." I said. But we both knew that was unlikely.

"What if it's one of us?" Mia spoke, softly.

I turned my head toward her, studying her face. Oddly enough, she was even prettier in the morning, her cheeks doughy and soft, not an ounce of makeup on her moon-like face.

"One of us. As in, you, me, Rob, Sammy, or Opal...? Why would we hurt Scarlett? She was our friend."

Mia tossed the covers aside, revealing a skimpy black bra and purple thongs. I had to look away—the edges of her body too perfect, too pretty ... the kind of beauty it hurts to look at.

"Not all of us are friends."

I knew what she meant—Opal had a reason to dislike Scarlett, obviously, if she had discovered she was hooking up with Rob behind her back...

"I don't think Opal is capable of that. Plus, Scarlett is so much bigger than her ... *was*. Was so much bigger, I should say. Scarlett could have taken her..." I said.

"Not if she snuck up on her." Mia stood up, exposing her backside. I looked away as she shimmied into a torn, paint-stained pair of Levis and a woolly old sweater two sizes too big.

I tried to imagine Opal, hiding out there on the island. Waiting to attack Scarlett with a knife in the dark.

"She came right to the kitchen during the fire, though, remember? I mean, she could have killed Scarlett and run back, faking it … but why would she do that? And she looked half-asleep if you ask me," I said.

"You're right, but I can't help wondering. I just can't believe she's gone."

"I know. Me too," I said, solemnly.

"We need to fix the boat today. That's my only priority," Mia said. She twisted her hair in a crooked knot at the base of her skull. "This was supposed to be a dream come true, you know. Me and you…? Sammy and Scarlett…" Mia's head drooped to her chest.

"And instead of a dream, what we have here is a nightmare," I said, finishing her thought.

Chapter Forty-Two

Mia

The house felt damp and strange, as I followed Riley downstairs. It was cold, the kind of cold that settles deep in your bones then takes up residence there, refusing to leave.

Riley stopped suddenly midway down, and I was pressed against her backside. "Someone left the front door open."

"What? No, we locked everything last night..."

"I guess someone's already up and went out—leaving the door open behind them..." Riley took a few steps further. I held onto her shoulders, letting her be my shield. *What if there's a killer inside the house?*

"It's fine. I don't see anyone," Riley said. She was right

—in the light of the day, the living room looked sunny and bright, inviting. *Killers don't lurk in the light of day, do they?*

We reached the bottom of the stairs when I heard a strange sound—whining and desperate, like the dying call of a wounded animal—coming from outside.

I pushed past Riley, striding toward the open door. I stepped out on the front porch, nearly barreling over the bloody lump on the ground outside.

I gasped, lunging back and clashing into Riley.

"What the hell?" Riley screamed.

The face was swollen and battered; head covered in blood.

"Oh my God." I leaned over, heart pounding in my chest, and as I did, the swollen lids lifted and Rob stared back at me, eyes wooden and empty.

Chapter Forty-Three

Sammy

It was the screams that did it. They ricocheted through my brain, jettisoning me from my heavy black dreams in bed.

At first, I thought I had imagined the screams. Desperately, I clutched the covers to my skin, rattled with fear. Rob was gone. Quickly, I remembered our fight last night ... him deciding to go back downstairs to Opal... *Oh shit.* Everything came rushing back ... a killer loose on the island ...

"Sammy!" Mia's voice cracked like a whip and I shot out of bed, ran through the hallway and leapt down the stairs.

"Sammy, help!" Mia screamed. As I barreled through the front door, I found her bent over another body—this time it was my brother Rob.

Chapter Forty-Four

Rob

I'd never been so happy to be surrounded by women in my life. Normally, women complicated my life—but today, they were my saviors.

I'm so lucky to be alive.

"Don't try to talk. Just drink." Sammy eased a bottle of water to my cracked and bloody lips. I took a small sip, then another and another. Water had never tasted so good.

"If he can talk, let him. We need to know who did this. And we need to know where Opal went…" Mia cried.

I was lying on the living room couch, a stack of pillows curled under my skull, my long legs dangling over the edge of the couch. Sammy and Mia knelt on the floor at my side. Riley watched me warily from where she sat on the loveseat.

I took another sip of the water and shook my head. "I don't know," I croaked, giving her an apologetic look.

"Did Opal do this to you?" Sammy's eyes were bright with rage. It had been a long time since I'd seen that old motherly fury in her. *Always looking out for me, always having my back... My sister is the only woman I've ever been able to count on.*

I shook my head again. "No way. Opal wouldn't do this ... and she couldn't. Whoever did this to me was strong."

"You kept saying 'knife' while we were carrying you in," Mia said softly. Her face was sheet-white with terror, and she was shaking, the old tremor she used to be embarrassed about on full display.

I swallowed hard, a dozen tiny needles in my throat. "Y-yes. They had a knife. I think they even swung it at me. But I don't think I have any stab wounds... They hit me over the head with something hard. I don't really know what it was... I blacked out." I reached for the water again, swallowing until the last drop was gone.

"I looked you over. I don't see any stab wounds. Most of the blood is coming from your head and face. Somebody whacked you good out there," Sammy said, through clenched teeth.

"I didn't see anyone out there though." Riley was standing at the window now, peering out fearfully.

"It was," I coughed hard, "right down by the boat dock, near the trees. I went out to smoke. They beat me and left me for dead out there all night ... but if they were smart, they would have finished the job."

"Well, I'm certainly glad they didn't. I'm quite sure who did this, too," Sammy sighed.

"Who?" I winced as a stab of pain behind my eye hit like a lightning bolt.

"I think Opal hit you because she thought you were coming out there to stop her from leaving. The boat is gone and so is she. Along with her pack and other belongings..." Sammy said.

"N-no, no way... Opal wouldn't do that. She wouldn't leave us all here, and the boat had holes," I croaked.

"She was the one with the duct tape, remember?" Mia said.

Even though I hurt Opal, she wouldn't do something like that... Would she? I closed my eyes, giving in to the pain for a little while, wishing I had something stronger to take it all away...

Chapter Forty-Five

Riley

The boat is gone. The tethers that held it in place are gone. Even Opal's chunky black bag with the saucy pins and buttons has disappeared.

As a group, we looked far and wide, scanning the sea … but there was no sign of the boat that only yesterday we had dragged up on the shore so that the resin could dry.

I pulled Opal's drawers open and shut. Peeked under the mattress and shook my head with a sigh.

The only sign Opal was ever here was the frumpy black blankets, the unmade bed, little balls of her hair on the pillow and between the sheets…

"There's no way she just left," Mia said. She was leaning against the door frame; she looked ten years older, eyes and forehead creased with stress.

"She was angry. She was out of her mind, upset over Rob, maybe..." I suggested.

"I don't think so. As pissed as she was at Rob, she's not stupid. Patching up the boat late at night on her own, with a possible killer on the loose ... stupid. And taking the boat out on her own ... well, that's just suicidal. It's not like a lake or pond out there—those waters are freakishly wild out there..." Mia exclaimed.

"You got a point there. But let's assume she's stupid. Let's assume she did all those things you're saying, despite her better judgment. Maybe this is good news. Maybe it means she's gone to get help, and someone will be coming back for us."

Mia stopped, gave me a look as though I were the stupid one, and paced up and down the hallway, restless legs knocking together. I'd never seen her like this.

"I'd ask if you're okay, but I know you're not," I said, quietly.

Mia frowned, stopping in front of the kitchen window. She winced at her own reflection, taking in the wispy bits of hair and half-moon circles beneath her eyes.

"I need to paint. It's what I do when I'm stressed out. I can't think straight in this house... We need a plan. We must get off this island. And I'm certainly not going to hold out hope that Opal went off to fetch help for us..."

"Why don't you go upstairs and change? I'll check on Sammy and Rob, then fetch us something to eat. After that, we'll search the island for Opal. Maybe she just went off to the cottage to be alone," I said.

Mia closed her eyes briefly, pressing her cheek against the glass as though she were listening for something. "If she did, then she's truly nuts. No way I'd be out there alone with a killer on the loose. Unless…"

"Unless what?"

"Unless it was Opal all along—she killed Scarlett and injured Rob, the two people she was pissed at. Then, knowing she'd get caught soon, she took off in the boat."

"Anything's possible, I guess," I said, skeptically.

After I listened to Mia shuffle up the stairs, I tiptoed down to the living room to check on Rob. He was still stretched out on the couch. Sammy had scooted the loveseat closer to his side, and she watched over him like a hawk.

"How's he doing?" I said, leaning in the doorway.

Sammy glanced up, saw it was me instead of Mia, then frowned.

"He's okay. Just resting. I mean, I know you shouldn't sleep after a concussion … but he was already passed out after being hit and he woke up after that… Do you think I should let him go to sleep, Riley?"

I came to her side, squatting on my haunches next to her chair. "We'll take turns watching him while he rests, just to make sure he's still breathing and not having any new pain. I think he got knocked out, and he'll be sore for a while … but I'm pretty sure he's going to be just fine," I told her.

I tried to sound reassuring, but I didn't have the answers

either. He seemed to be doing fine, as far as I could tell. My only experience with CPR and medical training had been in a lifeguard course I took fifteen years ago. I didn't remember a single second of it, quite honestly, those years of my youth still hazy.

A cool wet cloth lay draped over Rob's face. With his hands folded across his chest and his back stiff and straight, he looked almost like a corpse. It reminded me of Scarlett, and I had to look away from him.

"Where's Mia?"

"Upstairs. She needed some time to think."

"No. Hell no," Sammy's voice shook, "the last thing any of us needs is time alone. Go get her right now. We all need to stick together."

"I think she'll be more helpful if she takes a moment... She's traumatized, Sammy."

"Mia!" Sammy shouted through the hallway, chin tilted toward the stairs. "Can you come down here, please?"

"Yeah. We need to stick together, she's right," Rob moaned through the cloth, jolted awake by Sammy's shouts.

I shrank away from Sammy. I'd never realized how motherly—how bossy—she was, until we came to the island. In a school setting, she seemed like the smart one. Serious, bold, wise. But here, she was like a mother hen. Always pecking, driving us all batshit crazy.

"Mia!" she screamed again, voice rising to an unbearable level.

"I'll go get her." I stood up and took off for the stairs, eager to escape the siblings.

As I reached the upper level, I found the door to the room I'd been sharing with Mia closed. It was quiet, no sounds coming out. I imagined the soft tilt of her paint brush; those silent strokes creating the loudest art you've ever seen.

I stopped in front of Scarlett's half-open door, tempted to knock and call out her name. *She's gone. Dead, remember?*

I nudged the door open with my foot, looking around the room. The bed was neatly made, although obviously slept in. Scarlett's backpack lay half-open, clothes exploding from the top of it. Any minute now, I half-expected her to waltz in and collapse on the bed, ranting about some juicy piece of gossip she'd scooped up.

For a while, I was able to pretend that my life was normal—school, friends, a social life ... such a far cry from my lonely existence before. But, being here on the island, reality was setting in. None of us would be friends after this...

I inspected her things. Makeup, blouses, three trendy pairs of jeans. Nearly a dozen hair scrunchies in a purple bag.

There was nothing personal in her room, which seemed so unlike Scarlett.

The room smelled of her, fruity and sweet, the scent of her shampoo and body lotion lingering in the air.

I was about to leave when I had a sudden thought.

Where is her cell phone? I hadn't seen it among her things. *Maybe she tucked her phone underneath her pillow.* Finding Scarlett's cell phone seemed like a pointless aim, but still … *there might be something on there that is important to know.*

I lifted both pillows but found nothing. Impulsively, I bent down low next to the bed, peeking between the mattress and box spring.

There was a thick black journal squeezed between them. I slipped it out, quickly scanning its pages before tucking it in the back of my jeans.

Chapter Forty-Six

Mia

"Riley, is that you?" I leaned out my bedroom door, voice shaky as I called her name.

"Just me." Riley poked her head around the corner, then stepped out from Scarlett's bedroom.

"What were you doing in there?" I asked, suspiciously.

Riley sighed. "Snooping through her things, honestly. I don't know what I was hoping to find—answers, I suppose…"

I could feel the tears threatening to spring back, my throat tickling with them, but I took several deep breaths instead. "I want answers, too, Riley. I can't think of any reason why someone would want to kill her. Can you?"

Riley chewed on her bottom lip, thoughtful. "I mean, I

know she had drug problems ... but I can't see anything related to that following her all the way here."

I shook my head, forcing back thoughts of my friend. I tried to remember the good parts of her, not the partying and the drugs ... not the sneaking around with my ex.

"Let me show you something," I sighed.

I motioned her into the bedroom and pointed at my mid-sized easel. "It's a raft."

Riley walked over to my drawing, awestruck.

"You made this? But it's a sketch, you usually paint..."

"I didn't need paints this time. I wanted to come up with a schematic ... a plan for a raft. I know we came here to focus on our art, but it looks like we might need to use our skills to find a way off this island. I think we can do it..."

Riley nodded. "I do, too. But here's the thing: having a boat is all well and good, but what we really need is a motor. The mainland is ten miles from here. Even rowing non-stop, it's going to take us a while to get there, even if we don't run into problems."

My heart fluttered as I realized she was right. *It is a desperate plan, but what choice do we have at this point? I can't stay here on this eerie, claustrophobic island where someone is running loose and killing people!*

With the sketch of the raft folded in my pocket, I followed Riley back downstairs to join Sammy and Rob. I still couldn't get used to the idea of it being just the four of us. The house felt empty without Scarlett and Opal here, too.

"What's going on with them?" Riley whispered.

She was right. Rob and Sammy were acting strange, heads huddled together and whispering.

"Everything all right?" I called out, stepping off the bottom stair and strolling into the living room. Instantly, Rob and Sammy sat back from each other, close-lipped.

"What is it?" Riley pressed. "Did you remember something about your attacker?"

Rob frowned. "No, I wish. It's nothing like that... It's just ... well, you need to tell them, Sammy."

Sammy crossed her arms over her chest, giving her brother a thankless grin. "Mia already knows some anyway," she snapped, side-eyeing me. Immediately, I knew what she was referring to.

"Am I the only one out of the loop then?" Riley glanced around the room at each of us.

"Just tell her," I said, sitting down on the edge of the couch next to Rob's hairy feet. *Ew. What did I ever see in him?* I wondered.

"Everyone deserves to know the truth," Rob said, pinching his nostrils and closing his eyes, as though he were fending off a painful migraine.

"What truth?" Riley asked. She looked frightened, eyes beady and black like a baby bird.

I stared at Sammy. She mentioned her problems in the hotel room the night before we set sail for this place. I longed to know more myself, the details of her crime.

"Fine," Sammy groaned, "you all know that I work at the smoke shop, right?"

Riley shrugged. We all knew Sammy worked there, but Riley was new to the group.

"Anyway, I kind of stole some money. That's it. That's the big secret."

I rolled my eyes. Leave it to Sammy to downplay her own mistakes, even though she's the worst at calling others out for theirs.

"How much money are we talking?" Riley asked.

"Enough that I'm looking at jail time for it if they turn me in to the police."

Riley sighed. "I'm sorry, Sammy. I wish you would have told me sooner. But still, what does this have to do with Scarlett and Rob? Don't you think we should be focused on finding Opal and getting off this island first...?"

"Worrying about jail is the least of her problems," Rob said, solemnly, glancing over at Sammy to make sure she was okay with him telling her story. "The guy who owns the shop—well, he's not the gentle sort if you know what I mean. He wanted his fifty grand back, but of course, Sammy didn't have it."

"How did you spend fifty grand?" Riley gasped.

Sammy groaned. "Easily. I paid off some of my student loans and caught up on some other bills. It's not like I took the money and went to the mall."

"He threatened to hurt her, and me too, if she didn't return the money within forty-eight hours," Rob said.

Sammy nodded along, looking worriedly over at her brother on the couch.

"And I take it you didn't pay him back," Riley said, stiffly.

"Of course not. I couldn't afford to."

I would have given her the money. She knows that. It's sad that she would rather run away to an island and hide than ask me for the cash.

A thought came rushing in. "Do you think your boss is here? Do you think he followed you all the way to the island to kill you over the money?"

Sammy shrugged. "It sounds crazy, but it's certainly possible. And after what Rob told me yesterday, about never talking directly with Manny, I'm wondering if someone set me up to come here ... to get back at me for stealing the money."

"What do you mean, Rob never talked to Manny?" I asked, incredulously. This was my first time hearing that tidbit of news. "I thought his friend said it was okay to come here ... that no one used the island so we could. Yada yada yada..."

Sammy kicked off her sneakers and folded her legs up in the chair all the way to her chest, just like she used to do when we were kids. *When she was nervous,* I remembered.

"Tell them, Rob." Sammy waved dismissively at her brother.

"Look, Mia, I never actually talked to the guy. We haven't hung out in years. But we talked online, and we worked out the details over Facebook Messenger," Rob explained.

"Facebook Messenger?" I cried. "Oh my God, I feel like I'm in the damn *Twilight Zone*. How could you all be this stupid?"

"You *all*? What the fuck does that mean?" Sammy snapped.

"Oh, don't act like you're innocent in all this. Your shit is what got us in this mess in the first place," I snarled, pointing at Sammy.

"I know, Mia. I could have asked you and your precious famous mom for the money. But I'd rather steal than do that. Because I don't want their blood money. We all know it got you out of trouble it shouldn't have in your freshman year."

"Oh, fuck off, Sammy!"

"Guys. Guys. Please, stop." Riley stepped between the two of us, her voice rising for the first time since coming to the island. "All of this fighting isn't helping. We need to get Rob to a doctor, and we need to get the cops out here. The only way we can do this is by getting off this Godforsaken island. Nothing else matters at this point," she said.

We were all silent, focusing on the quiet leader in our group.

"She's right," I said, and Sammy nodded her agreement, untucking her legs from her chest.

"Well, I think you're all wrong. I think Opal will get help

and come back to save us," Rob said, draping the rag back over his face.

I wouldn't count on that, I thought, drily.

Chapter Forty-Seven

Sammy

With Rob safely locked in the house, I followed my friends to the first outbuilding. I knew it was empty, but still, we needed to check for Opal. If she was lying somewhere, hurt or dead, we needed to help her.

This time, I was wiser—I carried a sharp kitchen knife in the back of my jeans. Because there was always the chance that instead of Opal, we'd find my angry ex-boss or some crazy killer sneaking around the island waiting for us.

The thought of my misdeeds at work being the cause of all this—Scarlett dead, Rob hurt, Opal missing—was more than I could take. I needed to find a way to make up for it.

I won't let anyone hurt my brother or friends. Not anymore.

Chapter Forty-Eight

Rob

My stomach churned, either from the beans Sammy had forced me to eat earlier or from the concussion. It was hard to be sure. At this point, I could only pray that I didn't need to use the restroom, because getting up while this dizzy and trying to stumble through the house was a bad idea.

I'd assured the girls that I felt okay. That I'd be fine on my own while they searched the property. But my head was spinning, the room tilting on its side, the length between the floor and ceiling expanding and compressing, in sync.

I closed my eyes, eager to black out and sleep for a few hours, but every time I tried to rest I remembered the heavy blow on the top of my head, the crushing weight of my attacker's hands holding me down. *If he wanted to kill me, he would have. So why didn't he?*

Why kill Scarlett, but then let me live? Unless … it's someone trying to get to Sammy, and by hurting me, they knew she'd take the threat seriously and pay up their money. Maybe…?

But there was no chance in hell of that. Sammy had no money. Any money we ever had we spent. When she'd got her first batch of student loans, she blew most of it—buying clothes and a car for me, paying my pricey bill at rehab.

I should have been a better brother. It should be me out there right now, looking for a way off this island, not letting my sister wander out there, a potential killer on the loose…

I hope she's okay. If something happened to her, I wouldn't be able to go on.

At the sound of the front door opening, I felt a gush of relief in my chest. My stomach pains eased, my headache lifting. All I wanted was a cigarette and a few tokes.

"Did you all find anything?" I asked.

But when no one answered, I yanked the rag off my face.

"Who's there?" I croaked. Heavy footsteps approached.

A face leaned over the back of the couch, coming nose to nose with me. This time they weren't wearing a mask, but I recognized the eyes. That evil smile in the dark… Suddenly, I could remember everything that transpired before my attack last night.

"Why?" I asked, heart thrumming in my chest. But I never received an answer.

This time when my attacker lifted the knife, they were determined to finish the job.

Chapter Forty-Nine

Riley

The salt air clung to my lungs, heavy and damp, making it hard to breathe as we crossed the rugged terrain, making our way toward the first building. But I knew we wouldn't find anything there. Aside from our storage bins of supplies, and some of my light die-cutting tools, it was vacant. No Opal, and no signs she had ever been out here.

But I needed to show the girls my idea before nightfall. They needed to see it with their own eyes.

"I was thinking about the sketch you made this afternoon, and I had an idea," I called over my shoulder. Sammy and Mia trudged along behind me, neither speaking. Their words earlier had been angry and hurtful, cutting like razors, but I knew they would make up—we had no choice but to stick together now, no matter how heated and stressful things became.

"What is it? What's the plan?" Mia asked, her voice echoing around the bare concrete walls of the building.

"This." I held out my arms, indicating our supplies.

"What's 'this'?" Sammy asked, tiredly, rolling her eyes in Mia's direction as though I wouldn't notice. *The more I get to know these girls, the less I like, or trust, them.*

"There's some plywood here."

"I know where you're going with this, but we don't know the first thing about building a boat, Riley," Sammy said, dully. "Our best bet is putting out some sort of distress signal, making an SOS for passing boats to see."

"I haven't seen one boat out here though, have you?" Mia asked.

Sammy shot her an irritated look.

"You're right, Sammy. Wood doesn't always float. It depends on the ratio between weight and volume. But you know what will keep us afloat? These storage containers." I walked over to one and popped off the top, then I dumped it on its side, watching our brushes and paints as they tumbled to the cold, hard floor below.

Sammy laughed, bitterly. "So, we're going to float in storage bins on the choppy, dangerous Bering Sea. Is this really your fucking plan, Riley?" She clapped her hands together, cruelly.

"No." I lifted the empty storage bin and placed it

bottom-up on the floor. Then I picked up a sheet of plywood, securing it over the top. "See?"

Sammy obviously could *not* see. She groaned, turning her back to me, arms crossed haughtily over her chest.

"I get it." Mia looked down at the board and container, eyes brightening.

I knew she'd be the one to understand, I thought, tiredly.

"We can make a raft if we use all of the containers and sheets of wood; we have to build it," Mia breathed.

"I need some air," Sammy said. The door to the building slammed shut behind her.

"It's a great plan, Riley," Mia said, glancing around at the containers. "It might be our only way off this island if we don't find another way."

"Sammy hates me," I told her, taking in a deep breath.

"She'll come around. We'll put up an SOS sign too. Whatever it takes to get the fuck off this Godforsaken island," Mia said, firmly.

"I'll go talk to Sammy," I said, looking toward the door. "Probably not a good idea to leave her outside alone right now anyway, no matter how angry she is."

"Yeah. You talk to her. She's still pissed at me, too. I'm going to lay out all these containers and try to do some measurements."

"Okay."

Outside, I was relieved to find her close by. Sammy's back was pressed against the side of the building, cigarette in her hand.

"I didn't know you smoked."

Sammy took a long draw, then blew a ring of smoke in my face. I waved it away, patiently.

"Look. I know it's a crazy plan. But I feel like I have to do something to help us get off this island," I said.

"Yeah, especially as coming to this place was my idea," Sammy blew smoke from her nostrils like an angry bull, staring at the house.

"I can't believe she's dead," I said. Less than half a mile from here, Scarlett's lifeless body lay bloody and rotting under a tarp.

"I know. I can't either," Sammy said, her tough exterior softening.

"I found a journal in Scarlett's bedroom earlier," I said quietly, taking the book out from the back of my jeans to show her. "I don't know what it means, but…"

Sammy snatched it from between my fingertips, flipping through the musty cream pages compulsively.

She stopped. Held it up to the light, squinting. Suddenly, her eyes grew wide with fear. She snapped the book shut, then bent down and stuffed it inside her own pack. A flicker of irritation passed through me.

"We'll look at this later when we go inside," she told me.

Chapter Fifty

Mia

It was a crazy plan, building our own raft when we knew nothing about boats or sailing. But when it came to getting murdered on a deserted island versus taking our chances at sea, well … I'd rather lose my battle there than to a crazed killer.

Who could it be? And why?

My thoughts tumbled back to Sammy's story. *Why did she really take all that money? She could have asked me—my family had more than we knew what to do with.*

One by one, I emptied out the plastic storage bins. Our paints and tools and resins and molds … everything we'd once thought we needed on the island. This could have been an amazing trip. I wish we had never come to Alaska…

I turned each bin over, counting them. *Six, that's it.*

It had seemed like a lot on the way to the island, but now … it wasn't much for building a boat.

We can make it work, but this is going to be a narrow raft. Not like the luxurious one I drew an hour ago…

I could hear Riley and Sammy outside, talking in hushed voices by the door.

Walking over to the door, I nudged it open with the palm of my hand and looked out at them.

"Everything okay?"

Sammy made a little guttural noise and wouldn't look me in the eye.

"Riley?" I looked at her, trying to figure out what my friends weren't telling me.

But Riley shrugged. She looked younger in the dark, the lines of her face smooth and shadowy.

Riley cleared her throat. "If it's okay with you, I'd like to get to work on the planks and trying to figure out the best method for safely securing them to the containers. Why don't you and Sammy check out the cottage and see if you can find a way into that locked building at the backside of the island? Make sure Opal isn't hiding away from Rob out there somewhere, sulking?"

"No way. You can't stay in here alone," I said.

"I'll be fine. The door locks from the inside, remember? Plus, I think one of us should stay close to the house in case Rob needs help. I won't leave the building until you guys are done with your search," Riley promised.

I tried to look at Sammy, get her opinion on this plan, but still she wouldn't meet my gaze, still angry from my harsh words earlier probably.

"Okay," I relented. "But I want to help when I get back. I think it's a crazy plan, but it's so crazy that it might just work."

Chapter Fifty-One

Sammy

Shadows danced on the wall of the cottage. In the cold moonlight, it almost looked celestial, like it came straight from an old-timey storybook. It was a strange little house, old and sprawling, but someone had loved it once. Cream-colored walls with wallpaper decorated in tiny pink rose petals ... almost like it belonged to a child, or young girl, once upon a time.

Mia perched on the edge of the old bed, looking like a little girl lost in the forest. She had on an ill-fitting sweatshirt and thick black boots. Her ponytail had come loose, tiny threads of hair sticking to the corners of her cheeks and mouth.

"We need to get in that other building. It's probably

locked for a reason," Mia said, face cupped droopily in her hands.

"What sort of reason?"

"Expensive tools or boating equipment? A crazed killer…? Why else would it be locked?"

I shrugged. "You got a point. But there's something else going on here, Mia … something that involves Monroe and someone who has it in for us. You, specifically."

Mia's head shot up, face inquisitive. "Why the hell would you think that?"

"Riley found something in Scarlett's room," I said, shakily. "A book. Technically, a journal… It was hidden under her mattress."

"Okay … so?"

"Did Scarlett have any siblings that you know of? A sister, maybe?" I asked.

Mia frowned. "No, I don't think so. She mentioned being an only child, feeling spoiled but lonely when she was young… What's this all about, Sammy?"

I slipped my backpack from my shoulders and let it drop by my feet. Unzipping the front pouch, I fished out the thin leather journal I'd taken from Riley earlier.

"At first, I thought it was just an old book. That maybe Scarlett found it and forgot to tell us … but then, I started reading it…"

"Let me see it." Mia reached for the journal, expectantly.

I handed it over, collapsing on the bed beside her while I waited for her to see the words with her own two eyes.

"Elena Blackwater was the first to die." Mia read the words slowly, carefully.

Her eyes lifted from the page, rising to meet mine over the book.

"There's more," I said, breathless.

I watched Mia's cat-like eyes move from side to side as she reached a page in the middle. She read the words slowly, in silence, her lips moving as she read along. When she was done, she handed it back to me and I read them too:

I like to pretend Elena's off at college, studying creative writing like she planned. Meeting so many friends she can't keep count anymore. She's exhausted by her never-ending social calendar. On the weekdays, she studies hard —she likes to stay on the Dean's list. She wants to call more often ... she does ... but she's just too busy. On the weekends, she goes to the beach for inspiration. She stands at the edge of a rocky sea cliff, remembers her roots, taking in deep puffs of salty breath.

My sister wanted to be a writer. She is a writer. WAS.

I imagine that the ocean is bigger than it could ever be on paper. More majestic that it sounds in print. Her life too fulfilling, too joyful, to fill the pages of a flimsy book. She'll write something beyond her own vision ... something our mom and dad would have been proud of if they had lived.

My sister is larger than life. The better version of herself—in some ways, the better version of me.

This is the version I want—not the version she really is. Her body smashed to pieces, her head at the bottom of the canyon ... no, that's the version reserved for horror stories. Not the version I know.

Sometimes, I imagine that I am with her ... on those sunny beach weekends at college. We're sitting on the edge of that same cliff, legs dangling wildly over the edge.

"This water. This view. Doesn't it make you want to write, Elena?"

But my sister always shakes her head. "No, it doesn't. Because I want to enjoy the moment ... suck it all in. Live beyond the pages, in a world better than the ones I create on paper. Like this one. With you."

But like the characters in her stories, the ones she used to read to me every night when we were kids ... like those characters, this version isn't real. It's the one in my nightmares that lends truth to the story.

Elena stands on the cliff, pressing the tips of her toes to the edge of it. She looks healthy, glowing. The heroine of her own story, not the wrecked, broken body at the foot of a cliff. Not my beautiful, broken, dead sister ...

And right before I wake up from this fantasy, Elena stands on the tips of her toes and says, "This is my voyage now." Slowly, she bends her knees, and then she dives. I watch her, elegant and graceful, as she collides with the deep blue sea and keeps swimming.

"Is this some sort of sick joke?" Mia pointed at the book in her lap.

Stunned, I took the book from her hands, gripping it until my knuckles went white.

"Of course it isn't. Why the hell would I do something like that?"

"Because you're the only one of us who knows exactly what happened to Elena. I haven't talked about it with the others. Who wrote that? Did Elena have a sister or brother?"

I opened my mouth, but no words came.

"It was in Scarlett's room, right? So, she was writing that … planning some sort of sick joke, writing a story to make me look bad!" Mia exclaimed.

"I don't think so. I think someone else is on this island. Someone who lured us here, pretending to be my brother's friend Manny on Facebook. Someone who wants revenge for Elena."

"But"—Mia's face froze in fear—"I didn't mean to kill her. It was a fucking accident! Everybody knew that back then. In fact, most people at Monroe don't even know what really happened, don't remember…"

"I know. I know." I reached for Mia, wrapping my arms around her. Clutching her tight until she stopped quivering in my arms.

"It doesn't make any sense," Mia said, voice barely above a whisper. "It was an accident," she repeated. "An accident …"

"Someone doesn't think it was," I said, solemnly.

Chapter Fifty-Two

Mia

Money can't buy love—that's a stupid old adage, but it's also true. My family never hurt for money, and as a child, I wanted for nothing. My mother bought me all the clothes and dolls I wanted. And my father, when he was around, took me to expensive Broadway shows and the most exquisite restaurants.

But it was less like they were taking me, or treating me to these things... The toys were a distraction, the fancy trips were for them; I was just the little tag-a-long, the nuisance who stepped on the heels of the fabulous Cristal Ludlow.

I fell asleep in coat closets on school nights, at the trendiest parties in town. I wandered through crowds of fancy dresses and suits, no one even noticing I was there.

So, the saying is true—money can't buy love. But it can buy many things.

For instance, money can buy your freedom. Money can get you off the hook when it really counts.

And when I fucked up and killed a girl in my first year of college, my mummy's money got me off the hook in less than a couple months. Not only did I not get in trouble, but my entire record was wiped clean.

Not that it's a secret—most of the teachers and students at Monroe have heard the rumors.

I joined a sorority when I came to Monroe, as so many other girls did. But, unlike the others, I had my pick of them —who wouldn't want the famous Cristal Ludlow's daughter in their sorority? Most of the new recruits experienced some sort of hazing, but I was immediately welcomed into the fold as one of the leaders.

I didn't have to grovel to prove myself; my privilege was my ticket in.

Elena Blackwater wasn't the first girl I put in my trunk, but she was certainly the last. And she was the only one who died.

I didn't know she had a heart condition. I never meant to hurt her, let alone kill her.

The others wanted to cover it up, a stupid mistake, they said... I wasn't the one who threw her off the side of the cliff. But I might as well have been.

Those days between the time her body went over the cliff and the time she was found... those were the longest hours of my life. And when the cops showed up at my dorm room, asking questions about Elena, I caved.

I cried. I told the truth. I begged for their forgiveness. I put out my hands, waiting for the inevitable snapping of cuffs. I'm many things ... terrible things ... but I've never been a liar.

But that didn't happen.

My mother swooped in. My father too. Along with their two attorneys.

Don't worry, honey. It was an accident. You didn't mean any harm. You were pressured by the sorority, my father said. It was the first time he'd come to school to see me—not just college, but any school I'd ever attended. Volleyball games and clarinet concerts and art exhibits ... he never showed up for any of them. *And now here he is, rushing to my side when I'm in trouble, not when I'm doing something worth showing up for.*

They told me to let it go.

I was off the hook; I was lucky.

No one scolded me for my deed. It was a blip on the radar, an afterthought.

Monroe administrators swooped in and shut down the sorority house. I left school and moved back home. They didn't kick me out; in fact, they held my place, until I was ready and able to return.

A couple years later, I returned to Monroe, once again a freshman. And that's when I ran into my old friend Sammy and moved in with her. I told her about the incident, although she'd probably already heard about it.

She didn't seem to mind. Like the others, she assured me that it was a mistake. That I had to move on. Let it go…

But someone hasn't let it go.

Because here she is, the dead girl's name in loopy, cursive letters: *Elena Blackwater was the first to die.*

She was someone's sister … someone's family.

Finally, someone wants me to pay for what I did that night.

Elena was the first, but she certainly wouldn't be the last to die for my sins. *Many more will follow,* the writer had warned.

Scarlett's death, Opal gone, Rob's near-fatal attack … all of those only lead up to the killer's real target: me. All these incidents leading up to my own eventual death, and ultimately, revenge for murdering Elena Blackwater.

Chapter Fifty-Three

Riley

My face was flushed with excitement as I closed the front door behind me. I'd been working on the "raft" for nearly an hour; although it was a crazy plan, I was determined to make it work.

"Rob, are you doing okay?" I called out.

The living room was dark, Rob's long, hairy legs still dangling over the end. Shadows danced around the room, tall and menacing.

I crept forward, eager to find Sammy and Mia. I'd promised them I wouldn't leave the building until they got back, but when I shouted their names no one answered. They must have gone to explore the other buildings. *Maybe they got inside the locked one, finally.*

I pressed my palms on the back of the couch, quietly leaning over Rob to check on him.

"Rob." His eyes were closed, his body stock-still. For a moment, he really could have been sleeping…

But along his throat was a deep, dark gash, cut so deep that he was nearly decapitated. I opened my mouth to scream, but no sound came out.

Chapter Fifty-Four

Mia

The name Mia is actually short for Maria. I was named after my great-grandmother, who caressed the soles of strangers' feet and made warts disappear with her mind. At least that's how the story goes.

But the young girl who lived down the street from us —*Sammy*—had struggled with her Rs, and when she started shouting through the fence for "Mia" in the afternoons, I decided that I sort of liked Mia better.

When your mother is a free-spirited artist and your daddy's not around to care, nobody gives a damn if you change your name. I've been *Mia* ever since.

But now, for the first time in a long time, I was thinking about Maria. That perhaps if I had kept her name, she would have bestowed some of her mystical abilities upon me.

Oh, to rub my palms together, and cure the gashes in Scarlett's abdomen. To mutter a few nonsense words and make the boat come back.

And most of all if I could change anything … I'd bring back Elena Blackwater. Although I never talk about her, she's always with me. Her haunting eyes, the cold dead blue irises staring up at me from where she lay curled and twisted in the trunk. Her coal-black hair spread out like a fan around her face. A black halo of death. And the worst part was her mouth, lips spread open and wide, as though she had died screaming for help. *Help I didn't give her.*

I never heard her screams. I was too busy, jamming out to Nirvana while I pumped the gas, flinging her around curves going 70 mph. Laughing at my own power. Thrilled at my ability to impress the other girls. For once, someone was paying attention to me. Not my mother, but me.

I didn't know Elena had a heart condition. I didn't know she would die that day.

The girls had pulled that prank on recruits a hundred times, or so they said. And I'd driven the car during several other hazing events.

But that night with Elena was different.

And, as though what we had done wasn't enough … those pleading, ghost-white lips and the eerie eyes, blue as the sea … then there was the thump her body made as she hit the bottom of the ravine.

We have to throw her over. There's no other way. They'll take us to jail and shut down the sorority. She never should have joined if she had a heart condition. She knew what she was getting into.

I listened to the words and I let them toss her off the side of the cliff. I did nothing to stop her from dying, and I did nothing to protect the sanctity of her body after.

"Mia, look at me."

I tore my eyes away from the book; stared up at my oldest friend. Sammy knew me better than anyone, and although we never discussed Elena's death, she knew it was something I'd never got over.

"We need to go check on Riley and Rob. We've been sitting in this cottage for too long … We need to move. Riley's probably wondering where we are…"

My legs wobbled like Jell-O as I stood, the book light as a feather in my hand.

But heavy as a brick in my heart.

"It was an accident." My voice shook.

"I know. And whoever is doing this … whoever's fucking with us, I'm going to kill them, Mia. They won't get away with what they did to Scarlett. I won't let them."

I nodded, but no matter what she said I couldn't help wondering if this was karma. Finally, some consequences for my actions. *How many times had I waited for the hammer to fall, only to realize it was never coming…?*

"Ready?" Sammy said.

I gripped the book in my right hand, glancing once more around the long-abandoned cottage.

"I don't know where Scarlett found this book. But I'm sure someone wanted her to find it. Someone who wants to pay me back for what I did to their sister."

"I agree," Sammy said, peeking out the windows, fearfully. "But we need to go back…"

"Not yet," I said, firmly. "Not until we check out that other building, the one that's locked. The killer isn't in the house, or outside … but what if they're hiding out in that building? It's the only locked building on the island. We need to confront them before they sneak up on us. I can't lose any more people I love, Sammy. I can't lose you … and Opal … I don't even know the girl, but I have to know she's okay. We have to, Sammy."

Sammy pulled on her wool hat, tugging it low over her ears, then pushed her glasses up farther on her face. "Okay, let's go see what's in that other building," she said, resolutely.

Chapter Fifty-Five

Sammy

I wrapped my sweatshirt around my right fist and looked at Mia. "You sure about this?"

Mia nodded. "I'll do it if you don't want to."

"No, I will."

The door to the building was padlocked shut, but there were four windows, two on each side, and nothing could stop us from breaking them and going in.

"It's just so dark in there… I can't see a thing. Can you?"

"No. Let's hope there's electric inside," Mia said. I glanced over at my friend. Ever since I'd shown her the journal, her face had been deadpan and unrevealing. I'd been so afraid someone was after us because of my misdeeds, never considering it might have something to do with Mia's past…

I knew about Elena Blackwater, although the others didn't, and even though we never discussed the young girl's death, or the role Mia played in causing it, I knew how much it weighed on her. *You can't take a life like that and not feel the weight of it.*

But I never expected to hear her name again, least of all here on a deserted island thousands of miles from home.

I took a deep breath. "Okay. Watch my back, Mia."

Mia spun around wildly, remembering for the first time that we were alone and vulnerable, far from the main house on the island. She held a small knife in her hand. If push came to shove, she might be able to give an attacker a minor cut; but, in reality, the knife wasn't going to save us if the killer had a larger weapon. And based on Scarlett's wounds, he certainly did.

Tightening my fist, I drew back then punched the window. The glass cracked but didn't break, and I howled in pain, clutching my covered knuckles.

"Oh, for fuck's sake." Mia pushed me aside and started pounding on the window with the side of her fist until the glass broke free.

"Give me your shirt."

Stunned, I unwrapped it from my fist and tossed it over.

Using the thick material to guard her hand, Mia knocked shards of glass away, until she could slide her entire arm in the window and unfasten the lock.

Carefully, she raised the window, knocking away more

loose shards of glass. Then she lifted her leg, preparing to climb on over.

"Wait!" I hissed. "What if someone is in there, hiding out in the dark?"

"Then they better be ready," Mia said. I scrambled around for my flashlight as she disappeared through the hole.

"Wait..." I flicked the on switch and leaned in, shining my light around.

Mia was standing there in the darkness, her back turned to me, unmoving.

"Mia..." I swung my leg over the side and squirmed my way in, struggling to yank my heavy backpack through the window opening and past the toothy jagged chunks of glass.

As soon as I was in, I could see what had Mia so mesmerized.

Raising my flashlight to the wall, I stared at a life-sized mural of Elena Blackwater.

Chapter Fifty-Six

Mia

"It's some sort of fucking shrine," Sammy said, breathlessly, from behind me.

"I can see that." I took two tentative steps forward and pressed my fingers to the petal pink lips of Elena Blackwater. In this painting, she looked more alive than she did that night in the trunk of my car. Whoever had drawn this was a masterful artist; and it had taken someone a long time to paint it.

Sammy stepped up beside me. She, too, reached out and touched the painting of Elena's face.

"It's not wet," Sammy said, thoughtfully.

"No, of course not. Look here." I pointed at the cracks in the lines, the faded black strokes of her hair. "Whoever painted this did it a while ago. The paint is degraded. It's probably been here for years."

"But who? Why?"

"I don't know," I said. "But it was someone who loved her."

"Did she have any family you knew of?" Sammy pressed.

I shook my head, barely listening. I was hypnotized by the bright blue crystalline eyes. The carefully shaped nose and chiseled cheekbones. Elena had been beautiful once, until I stole her away from the world. Despite my fear of what was to come, I felt resolute—like I'd been brought to the island for a reason. Elena Blackwater was that very reason.

I didn't remember any mention of Elena's family. All I knew was that Elena was new to Monroe, like I was. Only it was different—she didn't have a famous mother or an automatic-in in the sorority.

"She moved here. There, I mean—to Monroe. But I never knew where she came from. I never read about her family in the papers…" I said wonderingly.

The painting went dark again, as Sammy moved her flashlight around the room. My eyes still pinned to the painting, I saw it different in the darkness… *The light and the dark, the side that no one sees when the world goes black… She's gone, hard to see, but she's still there … gone but not forgotten.*

"Oh my gosh, Mia. Check it out! There's all kinds of stuff in here."

I peeled my eyes away from Elena, to see what Sammy was seeing.

She was right. Not only were there oars and paddles, life jackets and fishing supplies, but in the far-right corner was an old rowboat on a trailer with a tiny motor attached.

"This is our way off the island, Mia! We will drag this down to the water and get the fuck out of here," Sammy said, beaming.

"Right."

I glanced back at Elena. Her eyes followed me in the dark, sad and accusatory.

"Did you hear me? This is a fucking miracle! Let's go tell Riley and Rob!"

Sammy was pulling my arm, forcing me to turn away from the gorgeous painting. Something about the art style was familiar, but I couldn't quite put my finger on it.

Chapter Fifty-Seven

Sammy

As excited as I was about finding a spare boat and supplies on the island, I couldn't shake the feeling of dread in my chest. Mia was acting weird, spacey and mopey, and I was still fearful that the killer was waiting for us somewhere off the footpath, waiting to pounce with his big mean knife.

As we neared the cottage, I tried not to look at the tarps, shining beneath the trees. It was hard to believe that Scarlett was somewhere underneath one of them, covered up and rotting. *Our beautiful friend is gone forever.*

"Stay close to me, okay? And keep an eye out. Tell me if you see anything or anybody." I locked my arm through Mia's, practically dragging her back to the house. *She has to snap out of this funk. Whoever is messing with her is doing a good job, because she's not herself right now. We need to focus on staying safe and getting home...*

"Sammy?" Mia lurched to a stop and my heart thudded like a jackhammer in my chest as I looked around for the killer.

"What? Why did you stop?" I hissed, seeing nothing lurking in the dark.

"If the killer isn't in the house or any of the buildings, then where are they hiding? They couldn't have disappeared."

Sighing, but trying to stay calm and patient for Mia's benefit, I said, "I don't know. But I promise that I'll keep us safe. There's safety in numbers and right now, the best thing we can do is get back inside with Rob and Riley."

"The killer is hiding somewhere," Mia whispered, but she moved forward, allowing me to lead her back down the path.

As we approached the backside of the main house, the hairs on the back of my neck stood up. I could feel someone out there, close by, moving through the trees.

I stopped, fiercely clutching Mia's arm in mine.

"What?" she hissed.

"There." I pointed at a long black shadow moving around the side of the house. As it grew nearer, I recognized Riley moving through dead patches of grass.

"What's that in her hand?" Mia whispered. I could feel her entire body trembling beside me, or was that mine?

Riley moved with stealth, silent as she crept along. In her hand was a sharp butcher's knife.

"What if the killer isn't hiding?" Mia said abruptly, her lips pressed to my ear. I shivered. "She isn't hiding out of sight; she's hiding among us," she said, pointing a finger at Riley.

Chapter Fifty-Eight

Riley

W hen I saw two blobby black shapes in the dark, I let out a sharp squeal of surprise.

"What the hell?" I squawked, pointing my knife at Mia and Sammy.

Sammy put her hands up and took a step back from me. Mia glanced from me to Sammy, then pointed at the knife in my hand.

"Oh." I dropped my arm and the knife to my side.

"What are you doing out here, creeping around with a knife?" Sammy's jaw was so tense, I could see it clicking through her cheek. Saying what I had to say next would only make things worse ... much worse.

"I'm looking for the killer. I thought I heard someone out here and..."

"And what?" Sammy demanded, still looking at the knife in my hand as though I might try to stab her with it.

"I'm so sorry, Sammy. It's Rob… Someone has murdered your brother," I told her.

Chapter Fifty-Nine

Mia

I tried to stop her, but she was too fast, and my boots were like suction cups as I stumbled through the mud and muck and patchy little bits of grass.

"Sammy, wait!"—my screams bouncing around in the wind, blowing back in my face like a cruel joke.

Riley was faster. She bypassed me, reaching Sammy before she could get to the front door.

"You don't want to see him this way, trust me ... you don't," Riley said as she tried to stop her. But there was no slowing down Sammy. Using both hands, she shoved Riley, knocking her to the ground as she barreled through the front door.

"You okay?" I hesitated, unsure whether I should stop and help Riley or go after my distraught friend.

"I'm fine… Just go. Go get her!" Riley waved me on.

"No. God, please, no," Sammy wailed. She was draped over her brother's body, shaking his shoulders and chest.

"Breathe, Robby, please just breathe," Sammy cried, cupping his face in her hands. But as I stepped closer in the room, I could see there was no coming back. His throat was cut, the wound deep and vicious. *Whoever killed him tried to saw his head clean off, oh my God…*

"Sammy…" Desperately, I reached for my friend, trying to hold her as she held onto Rob…

"Don't!" Sammy screamed, swinging around so sharply that her elbow caught the side of my face. I staggered back, holding my cheek, tears streaming down my face uncontrollably.

"Rob, please." Sammy rocked back and forth, never loosening her grip on her brother's shoulders.

Chapter Sixty

Riley

"She's nearly asleep," I whispered, pulling the door to the master bedroom shut behind me.

"Don't close it," Mia shouted. Then, lowering her voice, "None of us can be alone. Not even for a second."

"What if I need to pee?" It was a joke, but it sounded ridiculously insensitive and stupid as soon as the words left my mouth.

"Then I'll go with you," Mia said, flatly.

I pushed the door back open, glancing in once more at Sammy. She was white as a sheet tucked beneath the covers, eyes growing heavy as she stared at a spot on the wall.

As I passed the laundry room, I poked my head in and looked around for anyone and anything out of place.

"Shut that one. We need to keep all doors shut unless

we're in that room. That way we will hear it immediately if someone tries to sneak in, or get past us," Mia said.

I joined her at the kitchen table. Her legs were tucked up on the chair, long gangly arms wrapped around her knees. She was shaking.

"The Xanax is working for Sammy. Do you want me to get you one, too?" In a moment of panic, to calm Sammy down, I'd run upstairs and retrieved my pills that the doctor prescribed for the flight.

"No way. I need to keep my wits about me, and so do you," Mia said.

I nodded. She had a point there, although I was so wired that there was no way I'd be able to sleep or rest any time soon.

"What about him?" I cocked my head toward the arched entrance that led to the living room where Rob's bloody, lifeless body still lay.

"We could try to move him somewhere, I guess." Mia gnawed on her lower lip, face green and sickly.

I shook my head. "I think he's too heavy. The three of us could probably do it, but not just us two ... and I don't want Sammy to see him like that again."

"We should cover him with a sheet," Mia said.

"Right. But then one of us will have to go upstairs and get one. And I don't want to leave you here..."

"We could go together, but..."

"No. You can't leave Sammy either," I said, firmly.

"Wait." Mia's head popped up and she looked toward

the cabinets. "There's some table linens in a drawer. I saw them our first night here."

I pushed my chair back and stood up. "I think I did too."

Opening and closing drawers, I finally pulled out a large off-white tablecloth from the bottom drawer next to the dishwasher.

Mia stood up, shaky and off-balance, and steadied herself with one hand on the butcher-block table.

"I got this. You don't have to help." Both Sammy and Mia had a strong connection to Rob, but I barely knew him. Easier for me to deal with the body.

Mia opened her mouth as though she might protest, but then closed it and sat back down. Wordlessly, I carried the cloth into the living room and shook it open.

Trying not to look at the grotesque wound, I spread the cloth over his face and tugged it down until it covered most of his body. Try as I might, I couldn't get the cloth to fully cover his calves and feet.

He was still wearing socks, thick gray sporty ones, and I suddenly felt the urge to take them off for him. They looked scratchy and hot.

"I can't believe he's dead."

I started at the sound of Mia's voice. She stood in the door behind me, swaying from side to side as though she were drunk and not just traumatized.

"I know. I'm so sorry, Mia. I know he meant a lot to you."

"Do you?" She cocked her head to one side, studying me

in a way I'd never seen her do before. I felt a flutter of fear in my chest.

"Well, you told me that he broke your heart so I can only assume that you loved him once. So, I guess I do know," I said, unsure.

Mia nodded absently, glancing at the sheet that now covered Rob's body as though she could see straight through it.

"What were you doing outside, creeping around in the dark with a knife? Were you going to hurt me and Sammy?"

I froze. "Of course not. Why would you even ask me that, Mia?"

I pressed a hand to my chest, a bolt of anxiety tightening my chest and throat. *Who the hell does she think she is, accusing me like this?*

Mia cocked her head the other way, still searching my eyes for something I couldn't give.

"I don't have the answers, Mia. I don't know who killed him, and I don't know who killed Scarlett. It could have been anyone. We were all in our beds when Scarlett ... when that happened. Well, everyone except Rob who was going to meet her..."

But Mia still looked unsure, gnawing on the tips of her fingers now.

"Sammy and I were together the entire time. The only one who could have hurt Rob is you. Unless Opal is still out there, or some stranger..." Mia said. Her eyes were glowing in the dark, one eyebrow arched angrily at me. I'd never seen her look so … nasty.

"Why would I want to hurt Rob, huh? I barely knew the guy," I said.

"I don't know. That's what I'm trying to figure out."

"Well, like you said, you were with Sammy. And, even if you hadn't been, we know she wouldn't kill her own brother," I said.

Mia narrowed her eyes at me. "No, she wouldn't."

"The only person who has a reason to dislike Rob is you," I said, the words slipping out before I could stop them. It was true though: everyone knew how hung up on him she still was.

I expected Mia to yell, but instead she laughed. That deep, throaty chuckle of hers now sounding wicked and cruel.

"I won't lie. There were times when I wished him dead. He did more than break my heart; he ripped it out of my chest and stomped it into the ground. But even so … if given the chance, I would have taken him back. I'd take him back still. Because I love him," Mia said.

"I know you put those holes in the boat, Mia. I know it was you…"

If Mia were surprised that I'd called her out, she didn't show it.

I went on: "I saw your face that morning when we found the boat. You looked happy, and then when everyone started freaking out, I saw the guilt written on your face.

And did you really think I wouldn't know what caused those holes? You used my scratch awl. When I went in there the next day, I could see how marked up it was even though I bought it new before coming. And it was you, out there in the building, painting late at night by yourself the night before the boat went kaput."

Mia shrugged. "So what? That doesn't make me a murderer."

"Then I thought: maybe it's better if we can't leave the island for a while. Maybe Mia's intentions were good. It will give us time to work, really focus on the art... I assumed that's why you did it."

"Exactly," Mia said. "And with everything going on with Sammy, I knew she didn't want to deal with the police after finding that old skull ... but I had no idea that there was a killer on the loose, or I wouldn't have done it. And I'd never kill my best friend's brother, and I'd never do anything to Scarlett. I was so angry when I saw Rob with that stupid girl ... but even then, all I wanted to do was lie down and cry, not hurt him."

"Opal. The stupid girl's name is Opal."

"Opal," Mia repeated, a look of pure disgust on her face.

"Opal. What if *she* is behind this?" I said, wringing my hands and walking back and forth.

Mia looked around the room, paranoid. "We never found her body, but the boat is gone so she must have left..."

I shook my head, warily. "She easily could have pushed

the boat in the water and let it float away. That boat is probably sitting on the bottom of the ocean by now. It was dark and stormy last night, remember? The winds and the current would have carried it away in a second. What are the odds of her jumping in a boat that late at night in the dark and with zero help, and also during a storm?"

"She wouldn't. She'd be crazy to do that," Mia said, thoughtfully. She was chewing her lip again, hair a frazzled mess of tangles around her face. "She might still be on the island somewhere. She could be crazy…"

"But is she crazy enough to kill?" I asked, raising my brows.

Chapter Sixty-One

Mia

Opal had a reason to kill Rob. She had a reason to kill Scarlett too. They were hooking up behind her back, sneaking around the island... *But what does this have to do with Elena Blackwater?*

"Riley, have you heard of Elena Blackwater?" We were sitting at the table again, eating cold beans from a can. It seemed wrong to eat with Scarlett and Rob dead, and Sammy devastated in the next room, but hunger is a nasty thing: it doesn't care what's going on, it still shows up and lets you know it takes precedence over everything else.

Riley stared down at the table. Her hands were folded in front of her, her legs crossed properly underneath. She looked like a child, young and naïve, sitting there.

"Have you?" I pressed.

"Yes. I think most of the Monroe students have."

"Then you know I killed her," I said, bluntly.

Riley lifted her head, eyes on me. "Yes, I do. I know it was considered an accident; a sorority prank gone wrong."

"Well, whoever is doing all of this, Opal or some stranger, I think it has something to do with Elena. In fact, I know it does," I said, remembering that eerie mural in the locked building and the journal in Scarlett's room.

"What in the world would make you think that?" Riley asked, face scrunched up in confusion.

"That journal you found. Did you notice what it said inside?"

"Oh, did Sammy show you? No, I'd barely even had a chance to glance at it. I showed it to her, and she took it from me. Why?" Riley asked, perplexed.

"The first line was: 'Elena Blackwater was the first to die'. And there was more in it if you flipped through the pages and looked."

"I found it in Scarlett's room. Why would she write that?" Riley asked.

I shook my head. "It wasn't Scarlett's handwriting, at least I don't think it was. I'm pretty sure Scarlett found it on the island. Someone else brought it here. Someone who wanted me to find it."

"But why? Who?"

I shrugged. "Opal, maybe? I mean, what do we even know about her? She could be related to Elena, for all we know."

"We know nothing about her," Riley confirmed, slumping back in her seat. "Nothing at all."

"Sammy said that Rob never talked to Manny. He got a message from Manny on Facebook about the island and they worked out the details there. What if it was someone else, someone luring us here to the island ... someone using a profile with Manny's picture? That shit happens all the time online."

"I don't know," Riley said, "that all seems pretty far-fetched."

"I would have thought so too, but I found something else. A painting in that old locked building. It was a portrait of Elena, someone painted it there years ago. Someone who's been to the island before, perhaps someone who lived here... The journal mentions that Elena is the writer's sister. What if Opal is Elena's sister? What if all of this is some game to get to me?" I said.

Riley looked as baffled as I felt, thoughts spinning ceaselessly in my mind as I tried to piece it all together like an endless jigsaw puzzle.

"What do we do now?" Riley asked, breathily.

"We wait until morning and then we get the hell out of Dodge," I said.

"But it will take several days to get the raft built. Maybe longer..."

"Oh, I forgot to tell you the best part. We found an extra boat in that locked building. We'll need to inspect it carefully, make sure it's solid and the motor runs. But I think it's our safest bet to just get the hell out of here and contact the authorities on the mainland."

Riley's face was a mixture of relief and dread.

"That's the only good news we've had since we arrived here," she said, quietly.

Day Four

Chapter Sixty-Two

Sammy

When I opened my eyes, the sun was streaming in through the curtains creating shimmery dust prisms in the air. The friendly whistle of a chickadee outside made the corners of my lips tickle with pleasure.

But then reality came whirling back, slamming hard and fast as I bolted upright in bed.

"Rob!" I cried. I was in the master bedroom, the room as unfamiliar as any. I shoved the thick blankets aside and climbed out of bed. My head felt strange, fuzzy and full, and I remembered the pills Riley gave to calm me down last night.

Oh, Rob ... please tell me it was a nightmare.

As I peered down the long, empty hallway, I was hit by

the strangest sensation. The entire house felt like a tomb, the silence suffocating from the inside out.

"Mia? Riley?" I padded down the hall, thoughts shifting from my dead brother to the possibility that I might discover my friends both dead.

"She fell asleep like that."

I stopped in the kitchen, staring at Riley and Mia. They were both at the table, only Mia's head was down; she napped peacefully, her cheek pressed to the thick block of wood.

"Rob." I turned left, drifting into the living room. A blobby white ghost was on the couch, thick linen covering my brother's dead lifeless form underneath. Only his legs were exposed, his feet covered in the thick gray socks I bought him years ago when he was strung out and wandering around outside with tennis shoes and no socks.

I let out a sobbing gasp, covering my mouth with my hand.

"I'm so sorry." Riley was behind me now. Gently, she touched my shoulder with her hand. I stepped away from her, suspicious.

"I didn't do this. Mia accused me last night. I know how weird it looked when you all came up on the house, but I was trying to find out who did this. He was like this when I came inside from working on the raft, and I thought I heard someone … so I grabbed a knife from the kitchen, and I went outside to find them," Riley explained.

I studied Riley's face. She looked sweet and innocent.

Sincere. *But what did we really know about her? Next to nothing.*

"Have you been awake all night?" Riley's face, normally doughy and sweet, was creased with anxiety. She looked older than her years, worry lines crinkling like old cobwebs around her mouth. Seeing her like that, with no sleep and no makeup, felt wrong.

"I wanted to make sure no one tried to break in. Mia tried to stay up, but she was too exhausted. I've been watching her sleep." Riley nodded at our sleeping friend in the kitchen. Mia purred like a kitten, a slender rope of drool forming in the corner of her mouth.

I nodded, remembering our bizarre discovery in the building... That was before we discovered something worse: Rob.

"Thank you for covering him up."

Riley looked down. "I wish I could have done more. I wish I would have come over to the house sooner, maybe if I'd been here to interrupt..."

"Then your throat would be sliced open, too."

Riley winced.

"About last night ... seeing you outside with a knife in your hand, then finding Rob ... I wasn't thinking straight. I know you didn't kill him. There's some sort of psycho on the island, someone who is focused on punishing Mia for a mistake she made in her past. Someone who was here long before we came to the island."

"I know. Mia filled me in on the mural you all found of

Elena Blackwater. I just can't wrap my brain around it..." Riley said, perplexed.

"Someone lured Mia here to punish her, and they're knocking off her friends one by one."

"What do you know about Opal?" Riley asked, chewing on the nail of her thumb.

"Opal? Why?"

"Because Mia and I were talking last night... Who else had a motive to kill Rob and Scarlett? And who else is gone without a trace? And for all we know, she might have something to do with that Blackwater girl. Maybe they were sisters," Riley declared.

Opal. What if Opal never left? Out of sight, out of mind... I'd nearly forgotten about my brother's stupid little girlfriend.

"Honestly, nothing. I knew my brother was dating someone from the pizza place he works at. But he said little about her. I didn't even know he was bringing a date until we walked in and found them."

Riley nodded, as though I were confirming her own suspicions.

"We don't know where she's from, or even what her last name is. It could be Blackwater for all we know," Riley pondered.

I moved to the window overlooking the back of the house. There was a faint crack in the glass. I pressed my finger to it, enjoying the sharp flicker of pain as I moved it side to side.

In the light of day, the back of the island looked sunny

and serene. Glittery sparkles of dew glistened, remnants of the brief rain shower gone, and somewhere in the distance, I could see the sea-gray shape of the tarps, spread over my good friend's body...

How could a place that looked and sounded like paradise so quickly become a nightmare?

"You okay, Sammy?"

I shook my head. "I stole the money for Rob. He wanted so badly to go to college, to get his own place... Everything I've ever done was for him. And now he's dead."

"I'm so sorry. I truly am," Riley said.

I rubbed my finger over the crack, harder and faster this time. *No, I'm not okay. I'll never be okay again. My brother is dead. The only man I truly ever loved or cared for is gone from my life forever.*

"We need to wake up Mia. It's time to move that boat down to the water and get the hell off this island," I told Riley, my eyes penetrating deep into hers.

... ...

... ...

... ...

... ...

... ...

... ...

... ...

... ...

... ...

... ...

Chapter Sixty-Three

Mia

The boat rocked dangerously from side to side as first Riley, then Sammy, climbed in.

Please work. This must work...

We had carried it all the way down from the boat house to the dock, grunting and groaning, setting it down and picking it back up until we made it to our destination. Riley had checked the motor twice. It was running—a freaking miracle after all the bad luck we had suffered since arriving on Whisper Island.

We had filled the boat with life jackets and a few meager belongings to get us to the mainland. The rest of our stuff would have to wait until later.

I began untying the ropes when I remembered something. The journal. *I can't leave it behind! What if the*

killer hides the journal and dumps the bodies while we're gone?...
We'll never have proof our friends died, or what the motive
could be...

"Don't move. I have to grab something back at the house really quick," I told the girls.

"No!" Sammy screamed.

"Hell no," Riley agreed. "Just get in the boat, Mia. We'll come back for everything else later."

I shook my head. "It'll only take a second, I promise. Plus, I have the knife. I'll be fine."

They were shouting for me to stop as I turned on my heels, jogging down the dock back toward the house.

Chapter Sixty-Four

Sammy

"Should I follow her?"

Riley shook her head. "No, just wait. If she's not back in a couple minutes, we'll go after her. What could be so important that she had to go back? Doesn't she value her own life, or the life of others?"

I narrowed my eyes at Riley. She was normally so sweet and agreeable, but there was a spark of fire in her words this time. *We are all on edge and in fear for our lives,* I realized.

"I don't know, Riley. It must have been important. None of this is Mia's fault." I stared up at the house, seconds ticking by like hours as I waited for my friend to return.

I tried not to think about Rob, dead and alone on the couch. *What if something happens and I never make it back to him? Years from now, they'll find his rotting corpse, and Scarlett's* too, *and they'll never even know who they were. They won't know how much they were loved...*

My eyes burned with tears. *Don't cry. Not now. Not again. You have to get off this island. Rob would want you to protect yourself and your friends. You WILL make it back to him. You WILL have a proper burial for your brother and friend.*

"The motor won't start." My gaze shifted from the silent house to Riley. She was barely tugging on the pull cord. It wasn't making a sound.

"What the hell? It started earlier," I tried to stand up, but the boat rocked angrily, and I pitched forward, my face nearly connecting with Riley's kneecap.

"Careful," she huffed. She turned back to the motor, wiping buttery streams of sweat from her brow.

"I can't believe we're leaving after only four days," I said, glancing around the island that had looked so majestic in its early photos.

"Four days is a long time," Riley said.

"No, it's really not..." I kept watching for Mia, waiting for her to return. *Hurry the hell up, Mia.*

"I guess I'll just row us there. Don't worry, I can do it," Riley said, determinedly, turning away from the pull cord.

"Look. There's no way in hell you can row us ten miles to shore. It's stupid to even say that, Riley. We need the motor."

"Yes, I can," Riley stuck out her chin defiantly like a snotty child.

I rolled my eyes. "Whatever, Riley. I'll believe it when I see it."

Riley arched one eyebrow. "You don't think I can?"

"No, I don't," I snapped, peering around and shielding my eyes from the sun as I watched for Mia's return. *Should I go back in after her?*

"Watch me," Riley said.

"What?"

"Watch me," she said again, slow and determined. She picked up the heavy black oar in her hands. I'd barely turned back to look at her when she swung it straight toward my face.

Chapter Sixty-Five

Mia

S unshine streamed through the windows of the house.
If not for the dead body lying covered on the couch
and the fact that a killer was on the loose, it might appear
old and charming. I'd left the journal in the master
bedroom, sitting on the edge of the dresser.

It seemed stupid to come back for it, but I had to have it
—it contained so much pain on its pages. Pain I was
responsible for causing.

As I trotted through the hallway, I slowed down as I
passed the laundry room. I released a breath as I passed by;
no lunatics lurking in the shadows waiting to grab me. The
door to the master was half-open. Clutching the knife
tightly in my palm, I nudged it all the way open with my
foot.

The journal was still on the dresser, a dusty stream of sunlight making it glow. I looked around the room before entering, relieved to find it empty just as before.

As I walked over to retrieve the journal, my eyes cast down to the floor and I spotted something I hadn't noticed last night in the dark. Opal's ring, the owl with its jewels for eyes, rested on the floor next to the bed. *I guess she did leave something behind.*

I snatched up the journal and turned to leave. But, on second thought, I turned back to look at the ring. The owl's eyes glittered back at me, like a warning.

If Opal is the killer ... then maybe some of her DNA is on this ring. If the cops can't catch her, maybe they can at least get some of her DNA off it...

As I reached down to pick it up, I saw a flash of red from the corner of my eye. My first thought was Scarlett, but then, as I knelt to the floor, pressing my cheek to the wood, I came face to face with Opal.

I opened my mouth to scream but no sound came out. She stared back at me from under the bed, eyes unblinking. Her black messenger bag stuffed under her head like a pillow. And her lips... They were parted in a ghastly O.

She was naked, wrapped in a towel. Her neck was blue and purple, as though someone had squeezed the life out of her.

Someone did, I realized in horror.

Heart ricocheting in my chest, I leapt to my feet, still clutching the journal and ring. *Opal's been here the whole time*

... *lying dead beneath the bed*... *Oh my God oh my God oh my God*...

Opal never tried to leave the island... She didn't steal the boat and she didn't kill Scarlett and Rob...

I was running now, plowing past Rob's body on the couch and plummeting through the front door.

As I raced for the dock, I could see Riley standing on her feet, gripping an oar in both hands.

I skidded to a halt, several feet from the dock, watching the pair. *Could one of my friends be the killer?*

I took two steps forward and as I did, Riley swung the oar at Sammy's face, sending her flying out the back of the boat.

Chapter Sixty-Six

Riley

I turned around and grinned at Mia, showing all my teeth. My hands were still on the oar as Sammy's body smacked the water with a thud and went under. Mia was running now, straight for the dock.

I planted my feet firmly, ready to use the oar again, but she surprised me by running right past the boat. She dove headfirst into the water to save Sammy.

"Idiot." I tugged on the pull cord and the boat roared to life as I whisked away from Whisper Island.

Chapter Sixty-Seven

Mia

The icy cold water struck my skin like a bolt of lightning as I plunged beneath the choppy seas. For a moment, I could see nothing, a wall of velvety blackness, an endless tunnel below. But then I saw her, Sammy's arms outstretched like a bright white angel, eyes closed, hair floating like a halo around her as she sank deeper and deeper.

My lungs already screaming for air, I fought the urge to turn around and re-surface. *I have to get her before I lose her.*

Kicking my legs as hard as I could, I reached for her, sinking deeper and deeper, following my friend's lifeless body down into the bottomless pit below...

Chapter Sixty-Eight

Riley

As the island grew further and further away, I kept my eyes steady on the water, waiting for the women to resurface.

But they never did. Sammy was knocked unconscious by the oar, and trying to drag her body through these treacherous, deep waters was a suicide mission for Mia. *As self-centered as she is, would she really forfeit her own life to save her friend's? Doubtful, but not impossible.*

If she is dead, then I'm glad. But still ... it's not the death she deserved. And not the revenge I wanted for Elena.

Four days is a long time. It's how long my sister's body lay at the bottom of a ravine, waiting to be found by authorities.

By the time Elena was discovered, animals had ravaged her torso and limbs… In the end, all we had was her head.

As soon as the coast was clear, I could return to the island and dump the remaining bodies in the water, including the medical skull I purchased online to give them a scare. No one would ever know that the girls were gone; Sammy's entire family was dead, Opal was a useless punk who didn't stay in touch with her parents, and the only one who would notice Mia's absence was her batshit crazy mother.

Lucky for me, I had sent an email before we left port from Mia's phone, telling her mother that she had changed her mind and decided to take a solo tropical voyage to Mexico instead. Her mother hadn't even cared enough to respond.

And Scarlett … despite all her "friends" online, she was a nobody. No one would miss her at all, except maybe her dealers.

Things hadn't gone to plan; I'd wanted to kill Sammy and get Mia all on her own, torture her for a while in a deep, airless place like she did my sister in that trunk of hers. But when they saw me creeping around with that knife, they got suspicious. And every time I'd tried to slip away last night to take care of Sammy, Mia had jerked awake, refusing to leave my side.

I steered the boat in circles, remembering the way it dipped and pulled around curves. I remember how much Elena loved that dingy old boat. I'd tie a rope to the back with a tube on the end and ride around the sea, trying to throw her off.

We had inherited the land from our great-grandparents, the Blackwaters. Elena and I, along with our parents, had lived here until we were teenagers, completely isolated from the outside world, doing home school half the time and barely leaving the island except for occasional shopping trips with our mother.

But when my father died in a freak accident—his foot got snagged in a piece of rope and he went overboard—and we discovered Elena's heart condition, my mother gathered up my sister and me, and we left the island, with no plans to return. She said the island was dangerous … that my sister and I deserved a regular life, on land, closer to healthcare, and closer to the rest of our fellow Americans.

I didn't want to leave, but Elena did. My younger sister always had big dreams; she loved to write stories. *I want to write something beautiful and terrifying, like Shirley Jackson,* she once told me. Well, that never happened … but my sister's memory would live on like one of Jackson's stories, that's for sure.

We moved to Tennessee, a major culture shock, and I hated every minute of it. I hated the few friends I had, and I hated being so far away from the island. *We'll be happier here. Most importantly, we will be safer,* my mother said. But my mother had a fatal heart attack in Tennessee, and my sister was murdered at college. Worst of all, her killer never served a day in jail. Mia didn't lose her status; her mistake was swept under the rug, and she continued to live her glamorous, beautiful life with her kooky, famous mother, Cristal. Mia probably never lost a day of sleep over my sister losing her life.

When I applied to Monroe, I didn't plan on killing Mia. I wanted to see her, *smell her*, the girl who ruined my life. I didn't know how I'd meet her, but I would eventually. And so I watched her around campus. I followed her artistic endeavors online. I never expected Scarlett to dump Mia's friendship in my lap.

At that point, it felt like a sign—Elena's ghost, calling to me from the grave, telling me it was time to avenge her…

Chapter Sixty-Nine

Mia

The sea was so dark, like the bottomless pit to Hell had opened up beneath my feet. Sammy sank lower and lower, arms outstretched reaching for me. Suddenly, her eyes were open, wide and desperate, pleading... My fingers grazed hers, but then she was gone. And the body with its cruel needs fought against me. My lungs burned, my vision turning blurry and tunneled...

I dove deeper, desperate to save my friend.

I can't get to her. She's gone. I have to go up ... to breathe!

In that moment, my fear of losing Sammy was replaced with something I knew too well: self-preservation. I peered up at the ceiling of water above me, so far... *I'll never make it.*

I kicked as hard as my draining strength would allow, losing track of what was up and what was down, the sea like an hourglass, teasing me as I fought for my own life and mourned poor Sammy's...

Chapter Seventy

Riley

I didn't return until nightfall.

Out here, everything is forgotten. It doesn't whisper with ghosts—that's not why it's called Whisper Island. It's because it's forgotten, an afterthought ... it's not even on the map. A ghost, or an echo, of a place. A place I once called home.

Just like Elena, her loss ... only a whisper, an echo ... barely a blip on anyone's radar.

By the time I made it back to the dock and tied off, my legs were heavy with exhaustion. The excitement and tension of these last four days, and the month spent fantasizing about this trip, had taken their toll on me. Now, it was as though I were coming down from a delirious high, my body drained. My heart empty.

The house was dark, the windows in the front like watching eyes, the door a slash for a mouth, spreading open to swallow me whole.

I walked inside, stripped off my jean jacket and shoes, then waved at Rob's corpse on the sofa. I glanced at the pictures on the mantel... *Mia never even gave them a second glance. If she had, she might have recognized me, or my sister, two happy carefree girls ... whose world was stripped away from them in an instant because of her.*

I'd have to deal with the bodies tomorrow. It would be simple work, really—just a matter of using a wheelbarrow to haul them to their final performance spots.

I wonder if the sharks are dining on Sammy now, I thought.

In the master bedroom, I gave a silent hello to Opal underneath my bed, then went to the closet. It was empty the way I'd left it, but as I ducked down low inside it and waddled all the way to the right, I found the false panel my father had installed decades ago.

Back then, it was a place for hiding booze and cigarettes. Girlie magazines, and other trash.

Now it was my own little stockpile, but it had been nearly a year since I'd gone inside. It was a tight room, long and deep, but narrow on both sides. My tin cans of food, extra clothes, and hunting knives were stored inside.

"Home sweet home," I moaned, tugging on my sister's old Monroe sweatshirt. It was dank and oily, traces of the foul-smelling sea on the collar.

My temporary guests had been concerned about food,

but there was enough in here to get me through the winter if it had to.

I picked out cans of spaghetti hoops and broccoli cheese soup and carried them to the kitchen. I'd been unable to eat much at all since arriving on Whisper Island, but now I felt famished. The thought of filling my belly, taking a long bath, and sleeping eight hours sounded like heaven.

I knocked the cans together noisily, humming as I went to the kitchen to warm my food. The cold from the sea had sunk its talons into my bones, the chill so deep and brutal it would probably take a few days to shake it off.

I dumped the food into separate pots then turned on the gas burners, tapping my aching feet as I waited. My stomach churned, reminding me how long it had been since I'd eaten properly. *Tomorrow I'll take the boat out and do some fishing, pretend it's like the old days with Elena and me. And then, maybe I'll spend the night in the cottage.* I hated being inside the house, with the pictures and the memories... The cottage was Elena's and my place. We used to pretend it was our little dollhouse and we were the dolls ... with the delicate wallpaper and the books and our imagination... That was my favorite place on earth.

The events of the last four days played through my mind like an old home movie. Scarlett was annoyed when she found me, waiting out there in the dark. She'd confessed to me earlier in the night—a guilty conscience, I guess—that she was sneaking around with Rob. That closeness faded when I met up with her on the footpath, catching her unaware before her meeting with Rob.

What the fuck are you doing, Riley? It's too cold and dark to be out here all alone.

Scolding me like a small child, as though what was good enough for her wasn't okay for me. *Bitch.* The hunting knife was tucked in my belt. I split her open, doing it quickly and without much joy, like I would if I were gutting an animal for survival.

It's all business, I had told her, watching her eyes go wide with shock. She shook, bleeding out on the ground, eyes boring into mine as though she were asking: *why, why, why?*

Scarlett was pure business, nothing more. Of everyone on the island, besides that loser Opal, Scarlett was the least important to Mia. Knocking her off first would cause damage, but only minimal.

And I decided that hitting Rob with a steel pipe and letting him live for a while longer was good too ... Scarlett isn't the only one who enjoys theatrics. I enjoyed hitting him, and later when I slit his throat, I drew pleasure from that too. Rob was a vampire, sucking money and drugs and time and life out of everyone he encountered. *Good riddance.*

Opal, I barely knew the girl. I wanted to take her out first, but since she was hiding sick in her room so much that second day, I couldn't get her alone. But as soon as she was separated from her darling Rob, I took a chance. I found her naked and vulnerable, scared for her life. And that's when it dawned on me: Opal, out of sight and out of mind, running away from the island... She would make the perfect temporary patsy. I untied the boat, waving as it drifted away from the dock. *Bye bye, Opal,* I said. Although her body wasn't in the boat as I waved her on.

Things could have gone better. It's hard to control every variable, knowing when I could get them alone ... and I'd hoped that Mia or Sammy would find the journal first, not that junkie Scarlett. But no one is perfect; certainly not me.

I won and Mia Ludlow lost.

She was brilliant—brilliantly evil in her ability to go on, life as usual, with my sister dead and gone.

I glanced out the kitchen window, searching for her in the darkness. That's when I noticed a dull flicker of light coming from the old boat building. I dropped my stirring spoon on the counter and crept closer to the windowpane.

Did we leave the light on earlier when we were hauling the boat down to the dock?

I squinted in the dark, trying to look beyond my own fearful reflection staring back at me in the window.

No, I turned the light out when we left. I'm certain of it.

Quickly, I reached for the kitchen switch and turned it off, coating the kitchen in darkness. I flipped the burners off, too, then ran to get my knife. As I drifted through the rooms, I listened for noise. *Nothing. Just the ghost of my once happy family, haunting me for eternity.*

Taking a deep breath, I stepped out into the night, keeping the knife by my side.

The footpath was shrouded in darkness, the only sound the hoot of an owl. Its eyes followed me, watching eerily.

Finally, I reached the boat building. It only took a quick glance to spot her. She didn't appear to be hiding.

She had obviously climbed through the broken window again. This time, I took out my key and unlatched the padlock. As I closed the door behind me, she didn't turn around to look, as though she sensed me there and didn't mind it. I knew she'd be here, somewhere, waiting. *And then, finally, there were two.*

"What the hell are you doing, Mia?"

Mia moved the paint brush up and down, creating soft brush strokes over the face. Pale blue tears of summer.

"You painted her true to her likeness." Mia pointed her brush toward the mural of Elena, never turning to look at me.

When I said nothing, she added, "It's the best work you've ever done, Riley."

I smiled, although she couldn't see my expression in the dark.

"It's easy to create something brilliant when it means something. I've never been so devastated, so angry … as I was the day I painted her face," I said.

Mia nodded, but said nothing. Instead, she bent down, dipping her brush in a tiny tin can of blue paint. She continued drawing the face—it was a mixture of tan and blue, sadness and pain.

"I needed to make my own," she said, never stopping.

"So, you made a painting of your dead best friend next to my dead sister. Congratulations. Now, why are you still here?" I asked.

Finally, Mia turned to face me. Her face was pale and melancholy; she dried off her paintbrush on her shirt, then tucked it inside her jeans pocket.

"What was I supposed to do, Riley? Swim for help? Or wait until you went to bed and steal the boat?"

I shrugged. "That's what I would have done. The second one, I mean…"

"What's the point, though?" Mia turned around, reaching for her paints again.

"Stop painting on my fucking wall," I snarled.

Mia froze, brush caught mid-air, paint dripping off the horse hairs onto the concrete floor.

"I didn't mean to kill your sister, but I'm sure you already know that," Mia said. Her shoulders slumped, her chin falling to her chest.

"I could stab you right now." I pointed the tip of my knife at the back of her neck. When she didn't flinch, it enraged me. "I could cut you slow … taking my time, stealing your air piece by piece until you fade away just like my sister. And when you're dead and gone, I'll let the animals ravage your skin, then your bones, until all that's left is your pretty little arrogant head. I'll take that phony skull and toss it in the water, then replace it with yours. I'll display it like a trophy for all who come here. Here lies the world's most talented bitch! How does that sound, Mia?"

"If it makes you feel any better, I feel bad about what happened to your sister every single day. It's been eating me up inside..." Mia said.

"It doesn't make me feel better," I said, gripping the knife so tightly I could feel my knuckles trembling.

"So, you brought me here ... to what? Take away my friends, steal my life? Pay me back for you and yours..."

"That would be minor compared to what you did to me and my family." I coughed, lowering the knife as I spit on the ground. Paint fumes burned my mouth and nose.

"Well, let's go. I'm ready." Mia let the brush fall and clatter to the floor, and she spread her arms open wide.

"What the hell is wrong with you? You're nuts," I said.

Mia laughed, her whole mouth wide and toothy, and it vibrated around the empty building. *Still, as much as I hate her, it's a great laugh.*

"I'm the crazy one, you say... You're the one with the knife," Mia said, pointing.

"You are. I could never live with myself if I did that to someone. At least you deserve what's coming to you, Mia. Elena didn't. You're an evil, selfish, entitled bitch! And you should be sitting in prison right now."

Mia's mouth hardened into a grim line. "I agree. I should be. If you had killed me, then yeah ... I would have deserved it. But what about the others? Did Rob and Opal deserve it? Did Sammy? What about Scarlett, huh?"

"You are the company you keep," I huffed.

"What does that mean?"

"It means that they knew who you were, and they chose to be your friend anyway. Fuck all three of them," I growled. I imagined how good it would feel to raise the knife. To slash her pretty face to smithereens. *I'll make sure they never recognize her.*

"What about Opal? She didn't even know me."

"Opal was a mess. And she won't be missed. I knew plenty about Rob's life and his girlfriend before we got here. None of you were all that great. Sammy stealing money, Rob the junkie who was so easily conned into coming to the island by my phone messages ... and Scarlett, the attention whore. None of you will be missed. Especially you: the murderer who went scot-free."

"No one agrees with you more than me," Mia said.

Once again, she raised her arms, wild and reckless. "Come on. Let's get this shit over with. What are your plans for me? And for the record, nothing you do could be worse than what you've already done. The only man I ever loved is dead; my only friends are gone. You are gone to me ... and you were my friend, too."

"I was never your friend. I hate you more than anything, Mia Ludlow," I snarled.

"I might not have been your friend. But you were mine, Riley. You really were."

I laughed. "What a joke! Is that what you told my sister when you shoved her into your trunk? Promised her she could be your friend!"

Mia lowered her head, shaking it side to side. "It was a

joke. A prank... I had no idea she had heart problems. I didn't mean to..."

"It's too late for coulda woulda shoulda's, Mia. It's time to move. Go!" I pricked her cheek with the knife and yanked her by the shoulder, forcing her to come with me.

Chapter Seventy-One

Mia

I stood at the edge of the cliff, looking down at the water below, the sharp black rocks jutting out like incisors, ready to slice me to bits. Emotions whipped through me: guilt, regret ... but surprisingly, I felt no fear. Maybe a part of me always knew this day was coming—a day of reckoning for what I did to Elena.

At least it will be quick. I won't suffocate slowly like Elena did, or feel the breath stolen from my chest second by second like Sammy...

Riley stood beside me, feet level with the edge. She, too, stared down at the jagged rocks and water below.

"I really am sorry about Elena. You didn't deserve that ... and she didn't deserve to die. If I could take it all back and take her place … I would in a heartbeat." And I meant it. Every single word. I was guilty; my sins finally catching up with me.

There's no turning back now.

Riley looked over at me, expression softening. For a moment, I could almost believe she was still my friend … the gentle, kind, talented soul I'd met that first day in the pub.

"I love her. I wish she were still here," Riley said.

"Me too." I stared ahead, fixating on a passing bird, waiting for Riley to push me in.

Goodbye, world.

When seconds passed and nothing happened, I asked, "What now?"

When I looked over at Riley, she, too, looked lost, watching the same bird as me. I remembered the words in the journal, the words she must have written… She and Elena, in her fantasies, standing at the edge of a cliff. Just like this one.

As though she were thinking it too, Riley's lips spread into a wide grin. "I would love nothing more than to throw you from the edge. But you don't deserve freedom from guilt. You don't deserve that sort of death. I'd rather watch you wasting away in prison, the way it always should have been. They'll never find me, but they will find you. And this time … this time you're going to pay for what you did to my sister."

"Wait. Please don't…"

"This is my voyage now," she said. Then she leapt from the edge, crashing to the water below.

I screamed for her, but she was gone.

The Escape

Chapter Seventy-Two

Mia

I don't remember leaving Whisper Island. My last memory is boarding that ragged boat, pulling away, the island melting away behind me.

I don't remember stumbling to shore, or the doctors at the hospital who treated me for hypothermia. All I know is I made it, and none of my friends did.

I paid for my sins with more dead bodies, the way I always had.

Riley took everything from me, just as I did to her.

I thought my life would never go on; the press was persistent, cameras following me around for months asking questions. But just like they forgot about poor Elena Blackwater, they forgot about Riley's violent acts and the loss of Opal, Rob, Scarlett, and Sammy. They were just a blip on the press's radar. And no one blamed me. *Why doesn't anyone blame me?*

Every time I close my eyes, I see my best friend's face underwater. Her eyes popping open, desperately searching … begging for me to save her. But I couldn't. I couldn't save a single person except my own sorry ass, which seems to be a running theme in my life.

After speaking out about my crime and Riley's vengeance, the press still didn't vilify me. I think Riley hoped they would blame me for the others' deaths. She even went so far as to leave a note behind in my apartment … confirming my suspicions that this was her plan all along.

But life goes on. And Mommy's money saved me once again.

My paintings have sold all over the world, filling the walls of my lonely apartment instead of pictures of the ones I loved.

I often think about Riley. Why she killed herself instead of me that day. I think about Whisper Island.

For a few years, as I was busy with work and day-to-day life, those memories faded away. For a while, I nearly forgot. But then a reminder came, in the form of a sparkly gold box on my doorstep. There was no return address, but it was postmarked from Alaska.

It was topped with a shiny black bow.

Inside was a puzzle, a thousand pieces. My painting of

the island featured on the front; all those precisely cut pieces neatly folded in the cardboard box.

I looked everywhere for a label—where it came from, who made it.

But, deep down, I already knew.

I stuffed the puzzle in the back of my closet, burying it as deep as it would go, along with all my other secrets.

Chapter Seventy-Three

Riley

My biggest takeaway from the island came in the form of a lesson: it is much easier to hide in plain sight.

There were no pictures of me for the media to find—I'd refused to have a student ID photo taken when I joined Monroe, and all my identification on file was fake. And since I'd never joined social media, there was no trace of what I looked like online. As it turns out, my "connections", or lack thereof, helped me get further in life.

Elena and I had jumped off those cliffs a thousand times, squealing with delight on warm summer days. If you jumped in the right spot, from the right rock, you could land safely in the water, avoiding the sharp jagged rocks below.

It was stupid of me: letting her go. But I thought that maybe, just maybe, she would finally get blamed for murder. That she would finally be treated like the monster she was.

But no, not Mia Ludlow... Once again, with her wealth and status, she walked free.

I keep my hair shaved now, adorning my head with flowery turbans—no one questions it, assuming I'm a cancer survivor. And now that I've given up makeup, my edges and lines have given me a more mature, weathered look that I've grown to accept as my own.

I stand on the dock, feet firmly planted, waving my arms in greeting as the boat approaches.

My first group of tourists, six women and two men. They don't know that I chose them, specifically for this trip, targeting them with ads and letters, offering them a cheap deal to come to Whisper Island—one they couldn't refuse.

Another day, another person who got away with murder.

You'd think the horror of what happened here to those girls would scare them—but it's the opposite: the horror draws them in. *Damn vultures*. They can't look away from it now. There are people who flinch away from it; then there are those who are magnetized by other people's pain ... like a moth to a flame; they're only acting out of instinct, after all. Looking for carcasses to pick at, ways to make themselves feel better, more alive...

Mia deserved to die, or she at least deserved to be

punished. But there are some things that are worse than death—and Mia's own guilt and misery, the loss of her closest friends, was a better death sentence than taking her life that day on the island, I suppose.

As much as I hated her, the hole in my heart was connected to the hole in hers.

We were both dead already, as much as we didn't want to admit it.

I like to send her things, from time to time, to remind her I'm still here keeping an eye on her beautiful, privileged, joyless life. It gives me something to look forward to. I want her to keep me in the back of her mind: *I'm coming for you, Mia. Killing you softly and slowly, one day at a time...*

"Greetings!" The captain tosses a rope to me and I help secure the boat to the dock.

"I'm Maria," I tell them, offering my hand to the first handsome gentleman who steps out. "Welcome to Whisper Island. I think you're going to love it here."

I reach for the first heavy suitcase, but one of the young ladies puts out a hand to stop me. "That's too heavy. You'll never get it over the hull," she warns.

I smile politely, then say, "Watch me."

THE END

Don't miss *She Lied She Died*, another nail-biting thriller by Carissa Ann Lynch weaving a dark web of secrets around a fourteen-year-old girl who confesses to the brutal murder of a neighbor...

Get your copy today!

You will also love *The Invitation* by A.M. Castle, an unputdownable thriller following the reunion of thirteen friends on a small island off the coast of Cornwall and the chaos that ensues when the tide strands them and the murders begin...

Get your copy today!

Acknowledgments

The backbone of every triumph is built on two simple words: Watch me. In my case, no words have ever been truer. I fell in love with books before I could even read them, and I never thought I'd get the chance to be a writer. The first time I mentioned it, someone told me that writing isn't a job, it's a "hobby". I've spent many years trying to prove them wrong. The first time I tried writing a novel, I realized that it was the hardest thing I'd ever done. But that inner critic, telling me I'd never pull it off, pushed me to reach the end. And getting a book published is another huge hurdle that I was determined to get over despite the tough odds and naysayers. I'm grateful for anyone who has ever told me I couldn't do something because you gave birth to the "watch me" mantra that keeps me working hard every day. I want to sincerely thank my agent, Katie Shea Boutillier, and my editors, Charlotte Ledger and Bethan

Morgan, for letting me share my stories and giving me a platform to show them to readers. I also want to thank my copyeditor, Tony Russell, for your sharp eyes and your brilliant mind. You all are the ultimate dream team and there are not enough words in the English language to convey the amount of gratitude I feel for this team. I would also like to thank the entire HarperCollins and One More Chapter team for your encouragement and support at every turn. Thank you to my dear friend Chelsi Tauscher, who read this book first (unedited)—all I have to say is, "Chelsi, I need eyes on this book," and she's right there to offer her honest feedback and support. Chelsi, thank you for being my friend and the other member of our two-person book club. Thank you to my family for believing in me. And most of all, thank you to all my readers—I have the best job in the world because of you and I hope to keep you entertained for many years to come. Watch me try. xoxoxo

She Lied She Died

BY CARISSA ANN LYNCH

Now read on for an exclusive excerpt from *She Lied She Died…*

Best friend. Teenager. Murderer.

A young girl found dead in a neighbor's field. A fourteen-year-old who confesses. Just a child herself, could Chrissy Cornwall really be a cold-blooded killer?

Years later, the murderer is getting out and Natalie Bryers, unable to forget the night of Jenny's murder, still has questions.

Did Chrissy lie then or is she lying now? Did she really kill Jenny? And if so, will she kill again?

She Lied She Died: Chapter 1

I was nine years old when the murder happened.

Old enough to taste fresh-found fear in the air; young enough to feel unscathed by it.

Alone in the farmhouse, I squatted on my haunches in front of my brother Jack's bedroom window, eyes peeping over the ledge as far as they dared, faded binoculars shielding my face.

Jack would have killed me if he knew what I was doing because: 1. I was never allowed to enter his room, uninvited. 2. I'd gone through his trunk, which contained his "private things" (if you consider pics of naked girls with hairy bushes and a pair of binoculars, "private") and worst of all: 3. I'd "borrowed" those precious binoculars.

Jack was away, visiting with our dad's aunt, my quirky Great Aunt Lane. Six years my senior, Jack and I were as close as two siblings that spread apart in age could be, I guess.

But Jack's anger and disapproval about me being in his room were the farthest thing from my mind ... he wasn't here to stop me, and even if he was ... something important was happening, something that went above and beyond everyday sibling squabbles.

I'd been quarantined to my bedroom, courtesy of Mom and Dad.

"Don't come out until we tell you."

"We have an important meeting to tend to."

But *I knew*. I didn't know *what* exactly ... but I knew something bad had happened.

Sirens raged across the field, so loud my chest rumbled, thrumming in rhythm with the abhorrent beat.

My room—my temporary prison—was equipped with two windows, but unfortunately, both faced the trees. *Wrong side.*

I'd fought hard for this room—it was slightly smaller than my brother's, but the rich green view was superior, and it had a built-in bookshelf to boot. Now, for the first time, I regretted my choice.

The urgency and excitement ... that knocking fear ... that call of *importance*—all of it was coming from the other side of the house.

So, I'd crawled across the knotty pine floors, army-woman style, until I'd reached my brother's bedroom. It was unlocked, as was his precious trunk, and the binoculars were the prize I'd been hoping for.

I adjusted the binoculars on my face. They were old, too big for me. But they were my best bet because the chaos was happening across the field.

Through the foggy lens, I searched for my mother and father. But they were nowhere to be found.

There were others—several *others*, in fact. A cluster of people formed a strange, mystic circle in the center of the field, a cloud of low-slung fog forming a blanket around them. Like ancient druids, they were engaged in some sort of ritual...

I let my wild imagination run its course, then I readjusted my viewpoint.

The source of the sirens was obvious—an ambulance had pulled right through the center of Daddy's field, mowing down crops and kicking up mud. There were thick wet tire tracks in the soil.

The doors of the ambulance were left flung open on the driver's side and cab; the flash of the sirens glittered like rubies.

The circle-jerks weren't moving, but I could tell they were *looking*. *Looking at what, exactly?* I wondered. Heads ducked low, hands on hips ... there was one man with his hands folded behind his head. Another was a woman covering her mouth and nose...

My next thought—*a stupid one*—was that maybe there was one of those crop circles in Daddy's field. I'd read something about them in Jack's sci-fi magazine, the one with the grainy image of Nessie, with her long neck and protruding humps, on the cover. I hadn't believed a word of it.

As I trained the binoculars on the circle, willing the lens to focus, I realized that most of them were in uniform. *Cops. Boring!*

Suddenly, the man with his hands behind his head pivoted. He turned away from the others. Moving, *marching*, he was headed straight toward my house.

No, not the house … toward Mom and Dad. For the first time, I spotted them, huddled at the edge of the property. My dad, William, and my mother, Sophie. They looked too soft and young to be farmers. And, in reality, they weren't. Just two young people trying to have a place to call their own, to carry on a family tradition…

For the first time, they looked their age, faces grim and tight with worry.

Dad's hairy arm was draped over Mom's tiny, narrow shoulders. She was … *shaking*.

As the mysterious policeman crossed the field, trotting toward them, I was mesmerized by him … with his thick black hair and chiseled body, he looked scruffy and world-weary, but in a good way—like that actor in *Hollywood Detective*.

He stopped in front of Mom and Dad, hands resting on his waistband, fingers itching his gun like an outlaw from the Wild West.

Suddenly, he pointed across the field, gesturing wildly. Even behind a sheet of glass, I thought I heard Mom's sorrowful wail, "Oh noooo."

There was a gap in the circle now, I realized, pulling my eyes away from the cop and my parents. I zoomed in as far as the binoculars allowed, and for the first time, I could see inside the secret circle.

I could see what the fuss was about.

Knuckles white, I willed my hands not to shake. Willed myself not to look away…

There was a girl in the center of the circle. Fragile and small, she lay curled up on the ground, like one of those pill bugs we called "rollie pollies".

It wasn't natural, the way she was bent … arms and legs sharply curved and folded in, like a clay sculpture you could shape and mold, bend at will…

Could it be an alien … or better yet … a mannequin posed for a prank?

Sitting back on my haunches, I took a few deep breaths, then poked my head up again.

This time, the crowd had thinned out more, and as I zoomed in again … I saw her completely. For the first time, the lenses were crystal clear.

She was real—*human*. White skin, pale hair to match. Thin, white strands of hair blew around her face like corn silk. Her fingers were curled up by her mouth, nails painted matte black like the night sky.

Eyelids open, one gray eye bulged out at me like a grape

being squeezed between my thumb and forefinger …

The rolling in my stomach was less of a roll and more of a lurch. I was barely on my feet when the vomit came. It sprang from my mouth and nose, and although I tried, pathetically, to catch it in my hands, there was just too much of it.

I puked on my brother's favorite *Star Wars* blanket and CD tower, then I curled up on the floor like that *thing* in the field, trying to erase the image burned on the back of my eyelids.

It's not real. It's not real. Please tell me it's not real.

She Lied She Died: Chapter 2

Three truths.

One lie.

I've lived in the same shitty town for most of my life.

A girl named Jenny Juliott was murdered in my own "backyard".

I'm an aspiring writer who moonlights as a Kmart cashier.

Jenny Juliott's killer was never caught.

That original image of Jenny's face—moon-white and ominous in the early morning light—those bulgy eyeballs and dead gray irises ... *that* image had evolved over the years. Replaced by one replica after another ... *there is her face, the way I think I saw it that day ... and then there are the* memories, and later, the flashes of crime scene photos I pored over in my free time.

I didn't know her—of course I didn't; she was fourteen and I was nine. We may have lived in the same shitty town of Austin, Indiana, but we didn't know each other at all. Despite what they say about small towns, we do *not* all know each other.

But, over the years, I came to know everything about the girl with the white-blonde hair and the haunting gray eyes who smoked skinny cigarettes called Virginia Slims and who would never age a day over fourteen in the hearts and minds of Austin's residents.

Jenny Juliott had a mother, a father, and an older brother around Jack's age.

It was weeks before the crime scene was cleared from our property, reflective yellow caution tape stirring in the wind like a warning flag. Little bits of it floating around the property like confetti...

Years later, after the crime was solved and her killer was locked away in prison, I was digging around, looking for dandelions—not the yellow ones, but the ones you wish on —and I found what looked like a strip of gold in the dirt.

But it wasn't gold; far from it. It was that stupid old crime scene tape, bits of it still rotting around the edges of our property, still strung up in the branches of trees where it had gotten blown around that summer. *A reminder that it wasn't all a bad dream, as much as we wanted it to be...*

After Jenny was murdered, my parents pretended

nothing happened ... this was their way. That had *always* been their way. Perhaps they saw it as protecting me, but I saw it as treating me like an imbecile.

The lies we sometimes tell ourselves—or, in their case, lies were simply omissions.

"Nothing for you to worry about, dear."

"She was a wild girl, must have got caught up in some trouble."

"This is the safest town in three counties."

Lies.

Lies.

Lies.

Because the first thing my parents did was replace the locks on the front, back, and sides of the house. Days of riding my bike to my best friend Adrianna's were over. So were the days of slumber parties, playing outside alone, and walking to school or down to the park with friends.

Most of my friends, and their parents too, were too afraid to come to the farm. As though my family might be involved in her death, or that death itself might be contagious if you got too close.

There are two types of people in this world: those who drive by fast, avoiding the scene of a tragedy, and those who slow to a crawl, chicken heads bobbing up and down through the windows just to catch a glimpse of where a young girl died.

After the tragedy on the farm, we got a little of both

types. Those who wanted to avoid us, and the creeps who wouldn't leave us alone.

At school, there were stirrings ... I heard a few things, but since I was only in third grade at the time, a lot of the true grisly details were shielded from us.

But it didn't stop us from creating our own.

"Someone killed her. Hacked her up with a chainsaw. She must have pissed someone off right good."

"I heard aliens abducted her then dropped her down from the sky."

"They fed her to the pigs on the Breyas farm."

"Oink oink, Natalie. Oink oink."

Lies. All lies.

We didn't even own pigs, dammit.

It wasn't until I turned the ripe age of fourteen, the same age Jenny would have been, that I learned some things that *were* true.

Jenny Juliott wasn't killed on my family's farm—she was dumped there. She had been strangled and stabbed, and the police knew who did it, because the killer confessed: the confessor's name was Chrissy Cornwall.

Chrissy Cornwall: resident Austin tough girl who grew up on the "other side of the tracks". It just so happened that that "other side" was across the creek and through the woods from my family's farm.

Chrissy was fifteen when she committed the murder. She had jet-black hair, oddly streaked with flakes of gray at an early age—or was it white, like lightning? I couldn't be certain. I knew her even less than I knew Jenny.

Chrissy and Jenny were not friends; they didn't even attend the same school.

Chrissy was "homeschooled" by her mother—and by "homeschooled", I mean that they requested to teach her at home but never did. Unlike Jenny, who grew up in a nice middle-class home with a stay-at-home mother and a pastor father and attended Austin Middle School with most of the other kids in town, Chrissy was an outcast. An unknown.

Jenny bought ripped jeans from outlet malls and painted her nails black with twelve-dollar polish. Chrissy's pants were ripped with time, and from scrapping with her hoodlum brothers on the front lawn of her daddy's trailer lot.

Jenny was smart, pretty. Chrissy was … I don't know what you'd call her. Poor white trash, I guess.

On paper, Jenny and Chrissy had nothing in common. But there was one thread that tied them together, and that thread had a name: John Bishop.

John went to school with Jenny and the others, and he and Jenny were dating. But, unbeknownst to Jenny and the rest of the kids, John had a girl on the side—the dirty girl whose parents didn't send her to school, the girl with the strange black-gray hair who lived in a trailer.

And that trailer was a hop and a skip from my family's farm.

There were many people to blame for Chrissy's actions

—her parents for their lack of supervision and education, the state for not following up on reports of abuse, the school for letting a girl who didn't attend there kidnap another in the school parking lot...

But most of all, we blamed the guilty party: Chrissy herself.

She was jealous and angry, and determined to make Jenny pay for messing around with John, whom she felt she had a claim to.

Those are the scarecrow details.

Over the years, much more has come out. But some parts are still a mystery. I guess when it comes down to it ... you can never fully understand the heart of a person—why would anyone *kill* someone over a stupid boy? And to do it so brutally...

I hadn't thought about the case in over a decade. Chrissy had been tried and convicted, sentenced to life in prison despite her age at the time of the crime. I used to be obsessed, but not anymore.

The media had forgotten, as had I; we'd moved on to similar cases, ones with gorier details and more exciting bylines splashed across the nightly news.

But, of course, Austin hadn't forgotten. And as much as I tried to push it away, I hadn't let it go either. Jenny was always there; a memory, a warning ... a piece of my childhood I couldn't get back. Perhaps there was a small part of me that blamed her death for the fallout of my own childhood...

A lot can change in thirty years—but a lot can stay the same.

The third step on the corkscrew staircase still creaks when I step on it; the bathroom and cellar still stink of Clorox and mold like they did when Mom and Dad lived here.

Inheriting my family's farm ten years ago should have been a blessing, and when I was thirty, it had sort of felt like one. But thirty turned into thirty-five, and just last week, I celebrated my fortieth birthday the way I did my thirty-ninth—alone.

Wearing only socks and undies, I tiptoed from my room—my parents' former bedroom—and made my way for the stairs. Every light in the house was off, which was how I liked it. *If I can't see the shadows, then they can't see me...*

As I wound my way up the stairs, I caught a glimpse of moonlight through the picture windows in the kitchen ... *it can't be much later than two, maybe three, in the morning...*

So, what woke me?

There were sounds, but nothing unusual. The creaky old floorboards, the low hum of the refrigerator downstairs, the soft ticking of the grandfather clock in my office, which I'd converted from Jack's old bedroom.

Sometimes I caught glimpses of the place as it was before ... Mom in the living room reading paperback mysteries, Dad at the table with the *Times*, and Jack mounted up in the living room watching *Star Wars* ... their ghosts, just a flicker of movement, a light hollowed sound through the walls...

But there was something else this morning, something *real* ... whiny and synchronous, coming from the side of the house. And just like that, my legs were shorter and thinner ... I was nine years old again, creeping toward my brother's bedroom window, following the warning moans that lay beyond the dingy clapboard walls of my daddy's farmhouse.

It can't be. There's no reason for an ambulance ... no way there's anything out there. Maybe this is all a dream ... a memory...

The door to Jack's old bedroom was closed up tight. I'd like to think I kept it closed to ensure the privacy of my home office, but in truth, I think I did it out of habit.

Jack would want it that way.

I nudged the door open with my foot and, trancelike, I tiptoed toward the window facing the field.

When someone dies, it's not unusual for their family or friends to keep their rooms exactly as they once were. But with Jack ... I couldn't. Erasing him felt better, easier ... and so, the first thing I did when I moved back home ten years ago was tear out the carpet and take his old bedroom furniture out and replace it with a modern oak desk and shelves. A computer and a desk—the necessities for any writer. But I hadn't written a word in years.

As I edged closer to the window, there was no doubt: someone was out in the field. But that sound ... it wasn't sirens; no gaudy red rubies bouncing through the trees, ricocheting from my heart to my head.

But what I saw took my breath away.

A circle of people, each one holding a candle in front of them.

Thirty years later, and still: the first thing that comes to mind is a pagan ritual.

They were singing, something low and melancholy, flames from their candles casting ghoulish shadows over their faces.

I felt a flicker of rage. *How dare they waltz on my property like they own the place? This isn't a tourist attraction!*

But in a way it had been ... people had come from all over to see the "spot" the first few years after the murder. Sometimes, Dad would chase them off with a shotgun ... but after a while, he took to ignoring them. *"Easier that way,"* he told me.

But since I'd come home, there hadn't been a single unwanted visitor. *Until now.*

I'd assumed that most had forgotten Jenny Juliott and the girl who'd killed her.

Snapping the bolts to unlock the window, I shoved on the glass and poked my head all the way out, forgetting about my lacy black bra.

"Hey! What are you doing?" I shouted. It was windy, and chilly for October, and my words blew back angrily in my face.

I tried again. "Hello! It's, like, two in the morning..." I

screamed so loud I could feel veins protruding from my forehead.

And just like that, the singing stopped. Nearly a dozen heads turned my way.

"Hey, Natalie," came a woman's voice in the dark. As I squinted, she stepped into the sliver of moonlight in the field and pushed back the hood of a dark gray sweatshirt.

She looked familiar, but I couldn't place her. *Was she someone I went to school with?*

It's funny how over time every face looks familiar, but at the same time, I could never remember names. My childhood just a splotch on my memory board...

"Hey," I answered, dully.

Another woman stepped up beside the first. This one had black curls and, despite the chill in the air, she was wearing a white T-shirt and thin multi-colored yoga pants. A face I'd never forget: Adrianna Montgomery, forgotten friend turned local columnist. I tried to avoid her in town at all costs, but I saw her occasionally at the supermarket and Kmart when I was working. I usually pretended not to and luckily, she did the same.

"Natalie, it's good to see you. Sorry we're out here, but we tried to call you first ... we wanted to honor Jenny, especially considering the latest news. We can't forget what that monster did to her, you know?" Adrianna said.

The latest news?

My lousy paychecks from Kmart weren't enough to justify getting cable. I had just enough to eat, fill up my car with gas, and gas the tractor for cutting the field in the warmer months ... I didn't keep up with local news, or national news either.

"What news? I haven't seen it," I said, voice barely above a whisper.

The other faces in the crowd slowly materialized like old ghosts; I recognized a few of my former classmates and Jenny's brother in the crowd. My heart sank with guilt when I saw him. Although I'd seen most of the others around town, I hadn't seen him in years. I'd heard that he moved away.

As a kid, whenever Mom or I would see Jenny's family in town after the murder, we'd avert our eyes. Try to make ourselves invisible. Not because we blamed them, of course, but because we didn't know what to say ... *what can you say to someone who's lost a loved one that way?* And perhaps, there was also a nasty little sliver inside us, that selfish part that worried their tragedy might become ours. That somehow it was contagious ... in the same way people avoided me and my home because of what happened here...

Unfortunately for us, avoiding the Juliotts didn't do us any good because look at what happened to Jack.

So, as Mike Juliott stepped forward, I forced myself to meet his gaze. He was her brother—if anyone had a right to be here it was him.

Mike cleared his throat. "Didn't you hear? They're letting that monster out. Bitch got paroled. Chrissy Cornwall is coming home."

She Lied She Died: Chapter 3

Chrissy Cornwall is coming home. Five words I thought I'd never hear.

Mike Juliott's mid-morning announcement rolled over and back in my gullet as I scraped watery eggs onto my plate and buttered two pieces of toast.

It was Thursday, which meant I had the day off (a pretty shitty day to have off, I admit), but I was up early anyway.

No matter how late my mother stayed up at night, she always rose for the day by 5am. As a kid, her early-morning antics had irritated me no end—on weekends, I'd tried to sleep in, but then I'd hear her: banging pots in the kitchen, boiling tea by the light of the moon.

One time I asked her why she did it—*what is the point of it all?*

"I used to sleep in like you do, but then I realized that I feel

better about myself when I wake up early. There's no guilt, and it makes for a good night's rest."

At the time, it sounded stupid.

But as an adult, I understood.

There is nothing worse than lying in bed at night with regrets and getting up early to accomplish everything I need to do reduces that slightly.

I munched my toast, ate a spoonful of eggs, then chugged half a cup of coffee. There was a list of things I needed to do—grocery shopping, laundry, etc.

But all I could think about was Chrissy Cornwall.

Could it be true?

When they sentenced her to life, we all assumed that meant she would stay in prison for "life".

I understood why Mike was angry; he had every right to be. And the other people ... well, most of the townsfolk had children, and I could understand why they didn't want a murderer in town.

But my heart was in knots about it, my feelings mixed. Chrissy was fifteen when she got locked up. *That must make her, what? Forty-five or forty-six?*

Thinking back to who I was at fifteen versus who I was now ... so many things had changed.

But at the same time, nothing has.

I was still the same girl deep inside, only now my mousy brown hair was streaked with gray, my face a spider web of wrinkles and broken blood vessels.

And as I looked around the same dingy kitchen from my

childhood, with its peeling daisy wallpaper and cock-a-doodle-doo plaques on the wall ... I felt more certain than ever that time was standing still.

I'm still here. Still me. I never thought I would be stuck in the same place, but I am. And if I haven't changed much, has Chrissy? Do any of us ... really?

I left as soon as I had the chance, right after my high school graduation. I had big dreams of going to college and becoming a writer, and I fulfilled one of those—I worked a tough package-handling job that helped pay for my tiny apartment and covered the school expenses that my student loans didn't. I sacrificed my social life and moved to a college town in neighboring Kentucky where I had no family, no friends... I thought I'd have plenty of time for the fun stuff after college. But then Jack happened and somehow, I was back where I started—doing nothing with my degree, and just as lonely (if not more) here than I ever had been.

Yes, I had changed. It was hard not to after all that I'd gone through. And for the sake of Austin, I hoped Chrissy had changed too.

If she were really coming home, the town would be buzzing with it soon.

They already are, I realized, circling back to those ghoulish faces I'd seen in the field last night.

I scrubbed my dish and fork with soap and water, then left them to dry in the sink. Taking my coffee with me, I trudged up the stairs to my office. It had been so long since

I'd turned on my computer, since I'd felt the punchy feel of my keys.

I missed writing. But mostly, I missed the hope I'd held onto for so long—that one day I'd produce a great book. I wrote every night in my little apartment in Kentucky, mostly fiction—in the small gaps of time between work and school. I'd tried pitching some of my ideas to small publishers and agents, but without any luck.

Since coming home ten years ago, I'd been unable to write much of anything. Austin was, essentially, uninspiring.

My fingers glided effortlessly across the keyboard, typing Chrissy's name in the google search bar. I shivered despite the heat of my coffee—*is the furnace going out? Why is it so damn cold in October?*

It had been years since I'd checked up on Chrissy or researched the Juliott murder. As a teen and young adult, I'd been obsessed, and the invention of the internet had been both a blessing and a curse—it provided a wider window for my obsession and provided access to the horrors I'd tried—and failed—to forget.

The crime scene photos online were eerie. Some fake, but most of them real. And like the photos, the stories were a mix—conspiracy theories, repetitive summaries of the case. Podcasts and articles were helpful, and addictive, but the story was too complex for a six-paragraph op-ed.

It's not like the story hadn't been written—it had: *twice*. *Little Angel in the Field* and *Evil in Austin* had flown off the shelves. I'd dreamed of writing the story myself—*who better than me?*—but I'd never been able to get past the first few pages. After all, everything had already been written... *What more do I have to add to the discussion? And what do I really know about writing true crime?*

Several news articles filled my screen: the headline *Child Killer Released* caught my eye immediately.

Child Killer Released. It wasn't a lie exactly—but it was a double entendre. Yes, Chrissy had murdered a kid—but what the headline failed to capture was the fact that she had been a kid herself when she did it. Did the person writing this intend for the reader to feel confused? Is Chrissy a child killer, or a child who killed? *She's both*, I reminded myself. *Both.*

I scrolled and scrolled, reading more: *Jenny Juliott's Killer Released from Indiana Women's Prison.* I focused on another article instead, one with a more gripping headline: *Something Wicked This Way Comes: The Monster Returns to Austin.*

I clicked, immediately recognizing the article's author, Adrianna Montgomery: class president, town know-it-all, and senior columnist of the *Austin Gazette*.

She'd been standing in the dark amongst the others last night, her eyes judging me as they had for years...

Once upon a time, we had been best of friends. But that all changed after Jenny. Adrianna's parents had fallen into the category of people who tried to avoid our family and our house as much as possible. Adrianna was no longer allowed to come over, and at school, she avoided me there too. Even now, when I saw her in town, there was this wall between us ... something dark and hard. *Impenetrable.* I hated her for turning her back on me, for standing back while the others at school teased me about the farm and what happened there. And now, seeing her flourishing as a journalist made me cringe with jealousy.

I read the first few lines of her article:

It's been thirty years since the beloved Jenny Juliott was brutally sacrificed on the Breyas Farm. It feels like only yesterday to those who loved her. So, imagine the shock and outrage we all felt when we heard the news: Chrissy Cornwall is getting out of prison. What sort of failing system lets a monster like her out after only thirty years? Townspeople should take to the streets, petition the mayor—

I minimized the screen, rubbing my eyes in annoyance. The article was bullshit. Adrianna Montgomery had been my age when the murder happened. She didn't know the *beloved* Jenny any more than I did. And calling her murder a "sacrifice" made it sound like something from the occult. The murder didn't even happen on our property ... she was *dumped* here.

Any minute now, the field will be crawling with reporters ... hunting witches in Austin. Thanks a lot, Adrianna.

I clicked on another article, this one national news from

Crime Times. I waited for the grainy image to load, tapping the desk impatiently.

When it did, I gasped.

It was a split shot—on the left, a mugshot of Chrissy with her jet-black hair and hypnotic blue eyes. I'd seen this photo a million times over the years—she had grinned in her arrest photo, exposing gapped front teeth and her feral demeanor. Little shocks of white in her hair gave her an ethereal quality.

She looked like a maniac.

But the photo on the right was something else entirely ... it showed a middle-aged woman, with stringy salt-and-pepper hair and sad gunmetal-gray eyes being escorted out of prison. This time, when Chrissy's eyes met the camera, she hadn't smiled.

She looked downright sad and ashamed. Defeated.

I maximized the image, studying the woman that I hadn't seen in years—there had been a few photos from prison, but nothing in more than a decade. Supposedly, she had denied all interviews with the press after her trial.

There were no traces of the girl in the woman. *Where did she go?*

Her jowls were thicker, her chin whiskery ... and she'd put on nearly fifty pounds. It was hard to correlate the wild teen in the mug shot with this sad old woman beside her.

Skipping over the article itself, I typed in the search bar: Where is Chrissy Cornwall moving to in Austin.

I didn't expect to find an answer—surely, she'd try to

keep her address private. And I knew she wasn't moving back to her childhood home by the creek because it had been abandoned for years now, her deadbeat parents skipping town for good and local teens trashing the place during midnight drunk dares to visit the murderer's house...

But my search provided an immediate hit. Not only was her address online, but also the addresses for every living relative of hers in the country.

Someone had discovered her location, essentially doxing her.

4840 Willow Run Road.

Stunned, I settled back in my chair, reading the address over and over again. Not only was Chrissy coming home, but she was moving less than a mile from here. It made sense why she'd picked it; Austin was a small farming community, but most people lived in the center business district of town. She was moving to the outskirts near me—the place where outcasts reside.

Is she already there? Already moved in? I wondered. The thought of her being so close, breathing the same recycled air as me, made my stomach twist with unease.

I did another search, trying to figure out when she had been released exactly. I got an instant hit—*they let her out two days ago.*

Willow Run Road was a long road, but I guessed she was moving into one of the trailers people sold or rented out there. *Who is paying for her place?* I wondered. *Somebody must be.*

With a sideways glance out the window, I looked on as reporters grazed through my field like wide-eyed cows.

I didn't even hear them pull in.

A flash of cold white skin, those bulgy gray eyes...

I stood up and went to the window, lowering the blinds.

The monster is back.

But is she a monster ... or simply misunderstood? What truly motivated her crime that day? My thoughts were stuck on those two words: *child killer.*

Even now, a small part of me was filled with doubt. The violence of it ... it didn't seem like something a kid would do. It had never made sense to me.

Most of the conspiracy theories I'd read online were bogus—there were people who believed she was framed, some blaming her parents, Jenny's brother ... even a few who mentioned my brother or parents.

But her guilt was never in question. After all, she confessed to the crime.

And yet, I'd always felt like there was something more ... a missing link to the story. Something more than a silly crush on a boy had to have motivated such violence...

The media had lost interest in the case over the years, but I had a feeling with her recent release, the cycle would begin again.

If I'm going to write the story, now is the time.

But what is there to say that hasn't already been hashed over a million times? The only person who can tell me more is Chrissy herself.

Determinedly, I took a seat in front of the computer and pulled up Microsoft Word. I started typing a letter, but then, changing my mind, I opened a drawer, taking out thick tan sheets of stationery and a ballpoint pen.

Handwritten is more personal.

Head bent low, I began crafting a letter to a killer.

The chances of Chrissy Cornwall agreeing to speak with me were slim to none, but what did I have to lose?

So, imagine my surprise when, a few days later, she showed up at my front door.

Get your copy of *She Lied She Died* today to find out what happens next...